# THE SORCERESS EKEWANE

by

M.Rigoni

Illustrations by Benito M. Brancalion

Cover by Sandra Nooke

Although the characters within this book are fictional and do not specifically relate to any one culture, the story is intertwined with anthropological information, beliefs and legends from the people who still inhabit the islands of the Pacific.

First published 2013 by Marmolada Pty Ltd
ISBN: 978-0-9873544-1-9

# Contents

# Illustrations

By Sandra Noke

Cover. Ekewane - The Sorceress


By Benito Mario Brancalion

# Acknowledgements

There are always many people within our lives that help, support and guide us as we travel from one endeavour to another. It would be impossible for me to list everyone that has helped, supported and influenced me to write this book. However, I shall try and name some of those people that I think were instrumental to the completion of this book.

Sandra for creating a fantastic cover.

Carl and Mary, who originally persuaded and helped me to write a book on the customs, beliefs, legends and history of Nauru.

Clive who contributed with his knowledge of the Pacific Islands and the 'fresh food packs' he brought to us when we were living on the islands.

Don who first edited and discussed endlessly the myths and beliefs of people.

My editor Des whose help was crucial in editing the final manuscript.

Joe who finally got to format and see my book printed.

Adrian who helped with the editing and publication of the book.

My mother and brothers: John, Mirian; Johnny, Giulia; Anthony, Sharon; who have always been there for me.

To Susanna, Louis, and Marc.

My wonderful sons Adrian and Denis, whom together with their wives, TuQuan and Penny have always loved, supported, encouraged, and given me the most beautiful gifts of all, my grandchildren: Kiara, Aiden, Raquel, Dante and Poppy.

My husband Mario who has been there in my dreams and adventures and whose talent contributed to this book with his illustrations.
To the people of the islands who shared with me their stories and wonderful cultures.

To all of the above I thank you.

# Chapter One.
# The Voyage

Traditional Pacific Islander seafaring canoe

*It was long before Captain Cook sailed the globe and long before Ferdinand Magellan sailed the Pacific in 1519. It was long before Christopher Columbus found the new World of the Americas in 1492, that the people of the Pacific, explored thousands and thousands of kilometres of ocean, from the east coast of Asia across the vast*

*Pacific Ocean, from Korea to Hawaii, in frail outrigger boats with simple sails. Only the stars and strong ocean currents guided them.*

*These seafarers colonised and inhabited the islands of the archipelagos, known to us as the North and South Pacific.*

Ekewane had little room to move on the overcrowded canoe. Not that she had wanted to; she felt very weak and lethargic. She looked down at her legs that like the rest her body had become very thin and constantly ached. The cramps in her legs were especially bad and her knees were beginning to swell. She tried to massage them to help ease the pain, but the massaging action only brought little relief. Her hair once black and lustrous had started to become dry and brittle. Ekewane now spent most of her waking hours in that special part of her mind that allowed her to dream and drift back to the past. The pain was always there in the background, but she could escape the feeling of her body being gnawed by unseen hungry spirits.

It had not rained on their island for many years. The coconut trees had lost most of their leaves, and had only produced very few and small coconuts. The other trees like the pandanus, mango and wild almonds also suffered from the drought; many had either died or produced very little fruit.

The pigs that roamed freely around the village eating the old coconuts and were killed for festive occasions were very thin. The chickens that were traditionally plentiful were now also very few. They had either been eaten by the hungry islanders, or by the dogs that roamed the village. Even the fish, that had always been plentiful in the sea had disappeared. The fishermen had to travel further and further out to sea in order to find enough fish to eat. Some of them never returned.

The elders of the island had decided that some of their people must leave, so that the others could survive the long drought. Ekewane remembered the meetings that were held between all of the elders, and finally, although she did not know why, her family was amongst those that were chosen to leave. The elders had decided that members of many of the families would leave the island in search of another place to live.

Ekewane belonged to the Eilu clan. She was twelve years old and for all her life had lived in her village.

Her immediate family consisted of her mother Emanear; father Erangue, and brothers Enara eight, and Egui four. Her little brother Daboi who was only a baby, had died five days after leaving their island. Ekewane's family had lived with her grandparents, aunties, uncles and numerous cousins. She did not distinguish between her own siblings and cousins; they were one family as far as her clan was concerned.

The huts in which they lived formed a circle. In front of each hut were stones stacked in small heaps, these were the tombs of their ancestors, their guardians and protectors. A member of the family often left food and coconut milk beside these small tombstones. Some of the families buried their ancestors near the centre pole of their hut so that the ancestors' spirits still lived with them.

In the centre of the hamlet was a ring of various shaped and sized rocks, where a fire would be lit at night. Sometimes, meat would be cooked on it, whilst at other times it would be used to heat hot rocks that were then placed into wooden vessels filled with water, in order to heat it. However, for most nights it was a place for the adults to sit around and talk, whilst the children played nearby. Altogether the village was very large, as it was made up of the different hamlets belonging to the various families.

Ekewane did not know which hut was hers, because many families lived together in the bigger huts and the children kept sleeping in the different huts. In a way they were like different rooms of one big house. Tears filled her eyes as she remembered all the laughter and the games played with her cousins and the rest of the children of the village; but that seemed so long ago. Now all she could see was the vast expanse of sea; all she could hear was the sound of the waves beating against the canoe; all she felt was fear.

The canoe had been drifting for nearly seven weeks. Her father Erangue had asked her mother each day to cut a small mark on the side of the canoe; forty-six cuts were now visible.

She had seen the sun come up from the horizon, again, and again. Each time it rose, everyone looked over the endless miles of sea always hoping that the light would show some sign of land in the distance. But, each day brought only the flat blue sea and the hot scorching sun.

Ekewane had always loved the sun; after all, she was born on a tropical island where the sun shone for most of the year. But here on the canoe, the merciless sun had become their enemy. Their skins were no longer golden bronze but a strange burnt orange. Blisters had appeared on everyone's bodies; even though her mother and the other women had rubbed coconut oil over them, it did little to stop the blisters and the strange colour. Eventually, even the oil along with the food, the dried pandanus cakes, coconuts and other vegetables, had finished. They had been living only on the raw fish they were able to catch, and even though the men would often fish from the sides of the canoe, or dive deep into the dark blue sea, the fish were very scarce; they often went hungry.

It had rained on the fifteenth mark. Ekewane remembered, lots and lots of rain. At first everyone felt happy, and lifted their faces to let the rain cool their bodies and trickle down their parched throats, but soon the rain felt icy cold and painful as it slapped their hot burnt bodies.

The rain had turned into a severe storm as it often did in the Pacific, and the canoe was thrown in all directions; it was difficult to cling onto the sides as it went this way and that. The long awaited rain began to feel cold and threatening.

One of the other canoes still nearby, smashed in

half. The sails were swept away by the strong wind, and the outrigger shattered as if it was made of flimsy sticks.

Ekewane was too bewildered with terror to be able to shed any tears. They had helped the remaining members into their own canoe; they had been desperately clinging onto what had remained of their upturned craft against the winds, her father and the other men frantically rowed closer in order to reach them. Every now and again they would disappear under the towering waves. Their ancestors had looked down upon them and had helped save the stranded terrified survivors.

"Surely there are now too many people in this canoe!" she thought.

But somehow the long canoe they had built for this journey was able to stay afloat. Other canoes were also spared in the storm; she could see them in the distance. Even though the storm had brought with it the much-needed water, it was now running out yet again.

"Now that there are even more people on board, we do not have enough food and water for ourselves, "how can we survive? The people in the canoe thought. But they all knew they could not have abandoned the stranded members of their tribe.

When they had begun their journey there were ten people in their canoe. All of the other canoes also had ten to eleven people in each; the very small children under the age of two were not counted. The first two years of a child's life were the most dangerous. Small children often died before the age of two, so when a child turned two there was always a great celebration in the village. A pig was killed and cooked in an underground oven. The pig was covered with banana leaves, yams, and other vegetables wrapped in leaves. The oven was then covered with hot stones.

Ekewane remembered the excitement and happiness she and the other children felt on these occasions. They would get up as soon as the sun appeared and would help collect wood for the fire where the stones were heated. They would help the women wrap the yams and sago in banana leaves, and would watch the men dig a large hole in the ground oven and put the hot stones in it. Then the pig went in, and layer upon layer of vegetables would go on top. After which more hot stones would then cover the mound. She could still hear the singing and dancing that went on all night. Somehow, she knew she would never feel that carefree and happy again. Her years as a carefree child had ended.

"A storm is coming!" cried Emanear, her voice trembling.

Ekewane looked over the endless expansion of blue into the horizon. The threatening dark clouds were swiftly moving towards them at an incredible speed, and although it was hot and sticky, she moved trembling closer to her mother.

Her mind returned to the oncoming storm. The canoes had weathered the last storm; they were built to take them far away from their island. The canoes were built especially for this voyage with wood from the great tomano trees.

The men with axes made of large clamshells, had cut long wide planks. They then drilled small holes, and later using large needles made of bone had sewn them together with coconut rope. Glue, also made from the tomano tree, was used to make the canoe stronger. The outriggers were made from the hibiscus tree because the wood was much lighter. These canoes were more than twice the size of their normal fishing canoes. They were about 12 to 15 strides, and the boards were about four to four and a half hand spans so they were sturdier.

Ekewane remembered the women of the village had prepared dried pandanus preserves and cakes for the voyage. The pandanus cakes were usually made for pregnant women and she had never tasted them until now. But the elders had told the women to prepare them for the long journey.

The children in the village that were leaving were excited at the prospect of their new adventure. Many canoes had left the island; now only a few could be seen in the distance, and each day they became fainter and fainter on the horizon, it was hard to believe that she would not see her friends again.

Ekewane could not cry, her throat hurt from breathing the salty dry air. She knew that they had powerful magic in their canoe. They had dug up the remains of some of their ancestors, which were buried in front of her parents' hut; their spirits would be needed to help them survive the voyage and in their new lands. The ancient remains were carefully put into a fine woven casket and wrapped in an intricate mat with the patterns of her tribe; she had helped her mother weave the fine thread of the pandanus tree, into the patterns of her ancestors.

She knew that the other villagers had great respect

for her mother. Her mother Emanear had magical powers that were handed down to her through generations of the women of her family before her. Ekewane knew that she too would one day inherit this magic from her mother; she had already been shown the power of plants and flowers that helped heal many wounds. She felt a little better thinking of these things; it gave her courage to hope.

# Chapter Two.
## Leaving the island

*Shell armband*

There had not been any laughter or dancing in the village for a long time. The adults of the village had grown quiet; they only spoke in whispers. Only the children, who did not understand what was happening, played and swam as they always had.

Ekewane at the time did not comprehend why the adults were so serious; she and her friends that were chosen for the voyage were very excited at the prospect of the adventure. They huddled together at night and talked until dawn about what they would see and do in their new life. But they did not realize that they would never again see any of their families and friends that were left behind.

For many months the men were busy making the large canoes. The remaining families of the village gave those that left all of the food they could spare; it was going to be a long dangerous voyage.

Ekewane lay awake at night and listened to the elders talking about the island currents and how they would take the canoes to the neighbouring islands. They had heard of strange lands over the horizon. Passing islanders in their large canoes on their kula-ring, an exchange system that existed throughout the Pacific Islands, would tell stories of many islands where coconut trees and fish were plentiful.

Kula traders had over the years stopped at their island and exchanged *sopulava* -long necklaces of red-disk shells or colourful pink and orange coloured shells. Pigs, chickens, coconuts and other food, as well as crafts made from their islands were also exchanged; but nobody from their island had ever travelled far from their home.

These travellers would tell of strange lands and peoples. Ekewane and the other children were allowed to sit around the fire at night and listen to the wondrous stories told by these travellers.

Erangue, her father, held a position of power within the village and the kula-ring. He had the 'first-class' shell armband, and had a prestigious reputation throughout the islands.

Many of the villagers were jealous of this power, and looked at the shell armband with reverence and envy. Her father had carefully wrapped his precious shell armband in their tribal mat; he knew that if they landed on an island that was part of the kula-ring he would be given hospitality and protection, as well as the prestige indicated by his armband.

Ekewane now looked over the endless vastness of threatening sea that was quickly changing colour. She thought of her best friends Emarr and Amweb, and wondered what they were doing. She missed them, and although she was in the canoe with her family and cousins, felt lonely –lonely for the long days of fun with her friends. Although only weeks had passed she felt older. She looked down at her slim body and began to notice small differences.

"Perhaps, going so close towards the sun makes you older? So if I stay on the canoe for a long time I would end up old like my grandmother," she thought desperately.

Her father holding out in front of her a small piece of fish interrupted her thoughts.

"Eat."

Ekewane was not hungry, her body ached from sitting in one place for so long, and the hunger pains had now stopped; she thought less and less of food, as she and the rest of the occupants of the canoe became weaker and weaker.

"Eat!"

It was an order, so she slowly took the raw fish and put in into her mouth and slowly chewed. The chewing was painful, she could taste the blood from her gums and teeth that had become very sensitive, and so she swallowed. The food grazed her throat as it struggled to go down her parched, dry throat.

Ekewane kept watching the dark clouds. The sky had turned almost into night. Again she felt afraid. The waves swelled higher and higher. The wind was fierce and she thought that she would be blown out of the canoe; she did not have the strength to hold on much longer.

Ekewane's father fought the wind and made sure that the last remaining animals were all securely tied, and then helped the others in the canoe tie a rope around each other.

The boat was thrown from side to side by the furious waves, and all Ekewane could see was mountains of dark grey water; they lifted high above their large canoe and then came crashing down. She could no longer see the sky; only water. So she closed her eyes and dreamt she was back on her island, running along the beach and racing into the sea, swimming under the clear blue water to watch the tiny fish play amongst the corals.

She heard in the distance a whisper, a strange humming sound; a note amongst the crashing, howling rage of the angry sea. Ekewane knew that it was her mother chanting, she was working her magic. Ekewane again remembered her ancestors, they were powerful she thought, and so held onto a faint glimmer of courage.

Again and again she felt the canoe climb steadily then, drop violently back into the sea; somewhere deep within she knew that it could not continue to withstand the battering it was exposed to. She could hear her father's voice screaming above the crashing of the waves, he was screaming something, but Ekewane could not understand.

For how long she lay there numb with fear, neither awake nor asleep, she did not know. She concentrated on the laboured breathing of the small boy who lay close to her; in -out, in- out, in -out the breathing went. At some time however, she must have fallen asleep. The storm had ceased, and just as violently and swiftly as it came, it disappeared.

Ekewane was awakened by her father's intense voice.

"It's a frigate bird!" he yelled, unable to contain some of his anxiety.

Ekewane forced her eyes to slowly open, far above there was a black shadow of a large bird; she knew that the frigate bird could be a sign of land, but also remembered that it was also a sign of death. Frigate birds were said to carry the souls of those who died away; a pitch-black cloud would be seen on the horizon, they were the vehicles to transport the dead soul to the other world, and the frigate bird would accompany the soul.

She quickly glanced towards the horizon, but could not see any signs of clouds, so for a stunned moment, wondered if they had all died, and they were the ones being taken to the other world. The frigate bird was also a messenger from the spirit world, so everyone looked at her mother.

Emanear studied the bird for a long time until it was no longer visible, then slowly turned and said in a quiet voice:

"The frigate bird was sent by our ancestors. It does not bring with it a message of death, but of a new island, full of coconut trees and plentiful fish." She then lowered her head and started chanting.

A new wave of hope and excitement swept over the canoe. Everyone believed her, for she had the magic to speak to the spirit world. All eyes now were strained on the horizon; but there was nothing there but the shimmering endless blue of the sea.

Two more signs were cut into the board beside her mother, but nobody doubted that they would see the land spoken of by their ancestors. Then on the third morning there was what seemed a low-lying cloud on the horizon, and everyone knew that they had finally found land.

However, a new fear was taking hold; maybe hostile tribes inhabited this land, or those mythical spirits that could destroy entire villages lived there? There had been stories of such tribes and spirits told by some of the canoes that had visited their island.

Without any signal, the men on the canoe unwrapped their weapons. Ekewane knew that the people on the other canoes, when they saw the island would also prepare for a fight.

Erangue placed a clam-axe in front of her, she was stunned as usually only the men carried the weapons: she took the axe without questioning. She wondered how they would be able to protect themselves; they were all so weak. Again she felt the sharp pain in her stomach; the horrifying fear had returned again.

# Chapter Three.
## Volcanic Island

Volcanic Island.

Ekewane looked back from where they had come so as to see how many canoes were still in sight, but to her horror she could only see the endless blue flickering sea.

"The storm must have blown them off course," her father explained, as if reading her questioning gaze.

"They will find us again," he continued speaking mainly to himself.

She watched him as he gave instructions to stop the canoe. "Is he waiting for the other canoes?" she thought.

"We will wait until night so that we can see if there are any fires burning, then we will know if there are people here." Then to her surprise he slowly unwrapped his precious shell armband and fastened it around his arm.

The hours passed slowly as they drifted towards the distant land. Luckily the sea was smooth, only the ripples of the canoe disturbed the blue sheet of water. Her father took out a long rope and attached a large hook carved from the tomano tree. He then tied a stone that had a hole drilled in it, threaded some of their remaining fish on the hook, and dropped it from the side of the boat. The stone went deeper and deeper, but it did not touch the bottom.

"It's still very deep here!" he stated excitedly.

But no sooner had he dropped the line than he felt a sharp pull. "A fish!" he exclaimed.

The other two men climbed onto the outrigger and

watched as he pulled it in. It was a large tuna. Everyone forgot about the land. "Food!"

"The water here must be very rich with fish," smiled Gaida to one of the other men.

Erangue tossed the tuna into the canoe for the women to cut up and distribute; the soft inside of the fish was given to the smaller children. No sooner had he thrown the line back, and then pulled in again another tuna. They would now all have enough to eat, and the raw fish would also help quench their thirst.

Ekewane's father and the other men caught five more large tuna. The faraway shadow of the island did not seem so frightening now that they had eaten. But her father and the other men still wore a look of concern.

The darkness finally came. As in the tropics there is little twilight or dawn, one moment it seemed to Ekewane that she was watching the blue horizon and then it disappeared under the mantle of darkness. Her father and the other men then started to row silently towards the distant shadow. They did not have to tell anyone to be very quiet, they all knew that this should be the case; they were even too afraid to breathe out loud.

The two younger girls on the boat cradled the two

remaining small piglets closely. The piglets were treated like small children; they had been fed the same amount of food as the other children, but like the rest of the people on the canoe, had grown very thin and weak during the voyage.

As they came closer to the island they could smell it. The perfume of the tomano, and other flowering trees could be smelt even from far away. It was the familiar smell of home, and for a moment they all hoped that they might be home again. But as the canoe got closer to the island, there was nothing familiar about the outline. No pale soft sandy beaches could be seen, only a wide stony dark brown reef. At the centre of the island, reaching high above its surroundings was the outline of a dark mountain. Ekewane shivered, the sinister mountain looked dangerous.

"I wish we had returned home, this place has evil spirits," she reflected.

The canoe stopped bobbing up and down with the still water. All the occupants on the canoe were scanning the dark outline of the island, watching to see if they could see a flicker of light from a fire. But there was nothing. And still they waited.

Ekewane looked at the shadowy island and whispered, "Why aren't we landing?"

"We are not going to land tonight, there may be sharp rocks, and the waves could crash the canoe against them. We will land as soon as there is light." Her father's voice replied quietly.

So once again they waited. Ekewane was too afraid to sleep, "Perhaps we will be attacked by the people on the island. They could row out into the darkness. They know the beach."

She listened to the soft chants of her mother that soothed her, and felt the fine spray that floated off the sea which felt cool on her seared, hot skin. Finally, exhausted, she drifted off into a restless sleep. She dreamt that the island was full of the mystical beings that were often described by an elder of her tribe. She dreamt of the powerful mystical Ancient Spider, who in the beginning dwelt in darkness and was still living there in the dark mountain. The fear the mountain had instilled was now in her subconscious and fretful dreams.

Ekewane was awakened by the urgent whispers in the canoe. She sat up and saw the gold line on the horizon; it was daybreak and they had edged closer to the shore. Now she could see the outline of tall coconut trees, high pinnacles on the beach and the hovering mountain soaring above in the distance. She strained her eyes but still could not see any of the soft sandy beaches like the ones on her island; this place looked angry and jagged. She then looked around the canoe and could see a light mist enfolding it.

"It's my mother's magic protecting us," she thought, somewhat feeling better.

The men rowed silently towards the small bay and got out of the canoe as they were closer to the shoreline. Ekewane knew that they did this so that they could accompany the canoe safely to shore. She could now see the bottom of the ocean; it was a cold dark brown, not like the warm yellow of her island home.

"Ekewane get out and help bring in the canoe!" called out her father above the noise of the waves.

She leaned over the side and tipped herself out of the canoe expecting to feel a hard surface beneath her feet. But her legs felt strange and did not hold her up, and she sank. She struggled to stand up, but could not, her legs felt numb and she could not feel her body below her waist. She floated down as if in slow motion and watched the bubbles of air as they rose to the surface. She felt no fear, the warm water was familiar; her last thought was that it was rather strange to come all this way, and then drown in so little water. Suddenly two strong arms lifted her up.

"Hold onto the side until you can feel your legs again!" shouted her father.

She held onto the side of the canoe and instinctively tried to move her legs. It took some distance before she could feel the sharp bottom of the seabed then with difficulty, pushed her legs forward, one in front of the other like the others that were pulling the canoe.

So engrossed in the feeling of relief being able to feel her legs again, that she had momentarily forgot about the man eating tribes, and the mystical beings she had so feared. But a sharp cry from the dense forest sent shivers throughout her body and started trembling; the warm water now felt icy cold.

The others in the canoe also heard this strange piercing scream, and looked at where it had come from. The men seemed to ignore it and continued to pull the canoe towards the dry shoreline. The waves were now crashing against the canoe as it precariously kept its balance; they were losing it against the strength of the waves.

"Everyone get out and hold on!" yelled one of the men from the water.

Every person, except the very young glided silently from the canoe and held onto its side.

It took a long time to pull the canoe up the rocky sea barrier away from the sea. When they had finally succeeded, they all sat down exhausted and looked at their bloodied feet that had been cut by the rough limestone reef. Only the men looked around alert and prepared for any sudden movement.

For a very long time they all sat there. Her father eventually stood up and broke the solemn group.

"There are many coconut trees," he said pointing behind them, and smiled wearily "and the ground is full of coconuts. This island must not have many people living on it, because some of the coconuts are very old. We shall be able to live here; there seems plenty to eat. The sea is full of fish and there are many coconut trees."

Ekewane like the rest of the group knew that the coconut tree was a giver of life for islanders, they depended on it to survive.

"You boys climb up and cut down some fresh coconuts!" shouted one of the other men.

Ekewane did not question why the men did not climb the trees, she knew that they were still on guard; there could be some people living on this island and they did not know if they would be attacked or welcomed.

She stood up unsteadily, but did not know if her legs would be able to carry her.

Her younger brother and two of the other boys also staggered towards the high coconut trees.

Ekewane put the large clamshell axe inside her grass skirt and slowly started gathering the fallen coconuts. The ground still felt like it was moving, but she forced herself to walk and bend down. Her body at first felt stiff and painful, but after a while began to complete the action automatically.

She was halfway down in picking up a large coconut, when she froze; the high-pitched scream sounded louder. She looked over at the rest of their group to see their reaction.

Everyone had stopped what they were doing, and looked terrified. They looked in unison first at where the scream came from, and then slowly at Emanear. They all stood very still, waiting and listening attentively, but all they could hear was the sound of the waves crashing against the shoreline. They heard the scream again but further away this time, and then her mother's voice spoke very quietly.

"The spirits have seen us, but they will not harm us and have moved away."

Although everyone was still very fearful, Emanear's words helped reassure them and they continued working.

The men dug sharp stakes into the ground, whilst Ekewane and the other children continued collecting the numerous fallen coconuts. The women then hulled the coarse husks from the coconuts. The husks were carefully put to one side; the fibre would be needed, it would be twisted to make strings and ropes. These would be essential to build more canoes, houses, cages, fish traps and tie a spear blade to a wooden shaft.

Everyone helped pull the canoe up to the surrounding canopy and covered it with branches and leaves. They had found a small cave amongst the high limestone pinnacles, so took out all their meagre belongings and the few animals that remained, hid quietly in the cave-like shelter and waited.

The men decided that two of them would look around whilst the others stayed with the women and children to protect them. So they set off.

Ekewane and the others felt afraid for themselves and for the men that left, what if they did not return? But everyone kept this fear to themselves and sat quietly waiting. At least they had food to eat and coconut water to drink, so they felt a little better.

The men did not stay away very long they came back very excited. "We have found some water not far from here. It is not as sweet as our water at home, but we can drink it!" exclaimed one of the men.

"Water and coconuts!" we can live here they all thought. But deep down the fear of what was out there was still very much alive. They had food and water, but would they be able to live here without being attacked by other tribes, wild animals or the dark spirits? Emanear had said that the spirits they had heard that day would not harm them, but there may be other spirits on this island that would. Ekewane remembered again the Ancient Spider and shuddered.

Most of the water containers they had taken from their island were washed overboard during the storm. So the women quickly gathered the empty coconuts, attached them with ropes, and tied them evenly to both ends of a long stick that was used as a harness on the back of the men's necks. They had also found large empty shells along the beach, and these too were used to carry water. The containers were handed over to the men, who set off again to fill them with water.

It took only a little time before they returned again. Everyone felt some comfort knowing that there was water nearby, and took it in turns to drink the brackish water. It tasted a little salty, not sweet as the water from the rain or from the springs back on their island, but it quenched their thirst.

The day passed quickly and soon it was night again. No fires were set alight, as they were afraid to be seen.

The men again said they would go out to see if they could spot any lights.

Ekewane slept that night; there were no dreams in her sleep. So much had happened during the past few months, but now her bed was soft and cool, with the soft green leaves of the coconut tree. She could still hear the waves crashing against the shoreline, there was a cool breeze and the rocking of the canoe had finally stopped.

The men had come back during the night. They had walked a long way, always following the shoreline, but had not seen any tribes. Everyone felt better at this news. They did not know how big this island was, but there seemed to be no tribes nearby.

The following morning also brought another joyful surprise. As the people gazed out to sea they could see another canoe in the distance. The islanders recognised it as one of their own, because they could distinguish the outrigger on the right of the canoe, instead of the left side, which was more common with the other islanders.

Everyone waved and ran to the edge of the reef. Great cries of joy went up from the small group. The occupants on the canoe must have caught sight of them, and they too were overwhelmed with relief and joy.

As soon as the second canoe came closer the men swam out to help them pull it to safety. For the first time in a very long time everyone felt happier and hopeful. They would not be alone to face the mysteries the island might have.

## Chapter Four.
## Exploring the Island.

The members of the tribe sat around the fire near where they had landed.

"I think we should travel north along the shoreline and see if there are other people on this island. We have been here for many days, and travelled further and further around, but we cannot go safely any further away from the camp. We cannot risk leaving the rest of the tribe unprotected," explained Erangue.

"We will all go together." The men agreed.

The tribe had built small make-do huts from the coconut branches. That night it started to rain, so it was decided to wait until the sky cleared. It would be difficult enough for the women and children to walk around the reef without the fear of slipping on the sharp limestone reef, or not seeing the large occasional waves that could come up from the sea and sweep them away; so they waited patiently.

The soft rain did not dampen the moods of the people. The children kept gathering the fallen coconuts and some of the women were busy scraping out the flesh.

They would use the flesh to make milk and oil. When the tide was out, the women and children gathered periwinkles and other shellfish. When they had enough, they gathered dry leaves, lit a fire, and threw the shellfish on the open fire. Everyone gathered round talking and laughing; it was the first time they had laughed in a very long time. And although they were still fearful of what was on this island, they were grateful to their ancestors for helping them escape the perilous sea and lead them to this island, where food and water seemed plentiful.

The men however, took it in turns to keep watch nearby. Everyone felt happier since the second canoe had arrived, and went about their different tasks with more optimism.

The fierce scream shrieked out again, and everyone stood still as it echoed in the distance. Emanear looked towards the dark mountain, bowed her head and began to chant; everyone kept their eyes on her. The minutes ticked by but nobody moved, and only Emanear's monosyllable notes and the ocean waves could be heard. Finally she lifted her head.

"We need not have any fear, the mystical beings will not harm us. They have returned to the underworld where they live."

Everyone gave a last fleeting glance towards the dark mountain and continued, nervously, what they were doing before the interruption. Nobody questioned Emanear; they knew she could speak to the spirit world, but that did not prevent them from being afraid.

It had rained for another night. Softly it fell on their huts, and lulled them into a peaceful sleep. The next morning the sun was shining on the horizon. Everyone felt excited, for they now believed that others from their village could be somewhere on the island.

The chickens that had survived the long perilous voyage were still in their cages and carried. The young girls carried the piglets; they were still in charge of looking after them. When they were all assembled, they left the bay where they had landed, and slowly walked north.

Two of the men went on ahead of the group, scouting around in case there were hostile tribes waiting to ambush them. The men knew that if they were captured they could be killed and the women and children would become slaves or eaten, so they were alert to every noise and sound. They were fearful.

The tribe walked all morning. When the sun was

high in the sky they stopped to rest. Their feet were cut by the sharp reef, but nobody complained. The women gave out more coconut oil to rub on their bodies and especially the soles of their feet. When they had rested a while, they started walking again.

The coastline came out towards the sea and they looked behind them and could see the moon shaped bay where they had landed. And still they kept walking following the coastline.

By the time the sun was fading in the western horizon, the small assembly had decided to stop for the night. They were all tired and hungry, but the men did not allow them to light a fire.

"If there are people living on this side of the island, we cannot signal to them that we come in peace. We must meet them when there is light, " explained Erangue.

The fire was not needed to keep them warm, because the nights were very warm, but it pacified them, and they were reminded of home. It would also keep away any savage animals that could attack and eat them. The island seemed very big and they had only seen a small part of the coast.

The women and children gathered branches that

were plentiful, and laid them on the ground for beds. They built their encampment amongst the low-lying bushes that crouched along the shoreline, ate the raw fish and coconut flesh, and drank water from the coconut containers. The animals were also fed; there was plenty to eat now, so although they were tired and afraid of what may lie ahead, they felt better, stronger.

For how long Ekewane slept she did not know. In her dreams she was running along the sandy beach with her friends, when felt her body violently shaken, she wanted to scream, but a firm hand was placed over her mouth. Then she heard her father's whisper.

"Wake up and don't make any noise."

Ekewane knew not to ask questions and follow orders; she knew that her life and the lives of the tribe depended on following instructions, without needing to have explanations.

She quickly sat up and looked around. Her heart was thumping in her chest. She thought of the man-eating tribes, the mystical beings that lived on the island. The familiar feeling of fear that had not gone away since leaving her home, returned in force, leaving her breathless; she was afraid, for she knew they would never be woken up in the middle of the night if they were not in grave danger.

Everyone was hushed and looked towards the men. "There are fires further in the north." hissed Anweb. Everyone froze and looked around terrified, afraid they would be attacked at any moment.

The men walked away from the group and sat in a circle to decide what they should do next. Everyone else did not move and kept glancing at the dark forest that surrounded them. Apart from the whispering of the men, all that could be heard was the low chant of Ekewane's mother. The soft monosyllable notes always helped to calm the listeners.

But it was not long before the men stood up; a decision had been made.

"Ramanmada and I will go and see who has lit the fires. The other men will stay here and protect our tribe. Do not sleep and be on guard," warned Erangue.

Nobody spoke, and silently all the weapons were handed around to the women and older children. Ekewane still had her clamshell axe and held it tight. She was no longer considered a child; she now had her own weapon, on her island this honour would not have been given to her, it was only given to the boys, but here things would be different. So the group waited quietly: nobody spoke.

A golden streak of light could be seen out to sea. "The sun is waking up," thought Ekewane.

But there were still no signs of the two men. The small tribe huddled together feeling anxious for the safety of the two; there were only two of them, what if they had been attacked?

The sun was high in the sky and still they waited. Then a strange sound could be heard from a distance. Everybody strained to hear what this sound was; it was faint, but it sounded like laughter! The sound became louder and louder, it was laughter! The group looked at each other confused. Emanear smiled.

"It's Erangue, and there are others with him," she said.

All eyes looked at where the noises were getting louder. From a distance they could see four men walking along the reef. Curious to see whom the other people were, the group got up and walked quickly towards the distant men. As they came closer they recognised the other men, they were from the Deib clan. Instantly a great shout of joy rang out and everyone started running towards the newcomers; another canoe had been saved!

Everyone packed up their belongings and excitedly walked along the beach towards the third canoe.

That night there was reason for celebration, they did not kill a pig but the mood was happier and more excited than it had been until now.

"Maybe, other canoes have also landed, we will continue to look for them," they all said.

The next morning the group now much larger set off again. There were many more men now, so they were less afraid if they were attacked. Ekewane looked at her father proudly walking in front of the group with some of the other men. He was still wearing his shell armband. She knew that this armband brought her father prestige, but wondered why he was wearing it now?

The group walked all day and as the sun was setting they could see another group of people gathered on the reef. This time they were not afraid. They shouted and waved as they ran towards the group, for they had recognised the friends from one of the other canoes.

For many weeks the islanders travelled around the island, but did not see any more of the missing canoes. When they finally reached their initial landing place, the canoe was still there untouched, so the tribe decided that no other tribes lived around the coast. However, they could still see the dark mountain surrounded by a thick impenetrable forest, and knew that there could be still many dangers on the island.

The tribes talked increasingly of the dark hovering mountain; sooner or later they would have to go up there, but the mountain looked dangerous and unapproachable.

Ekewane looked up and could see many birds flying over the dense forest, they had not eaten meat for a very long time, and the chickens and pigs that had survived the journey were needed to produce more of their kind. So the birds looked very tempting.

"Perhaps I could go just a little way up the mountain and find their nests, " she thought to herself.

She knew that it was not her role to go hunting birds, or go were the men still had not gone.

"But nobody said we cannot go, things are different here on this island, there are not enough men and I now have my own axe," she reasoned to herself.

This thought kept going through her mind and every day she would go further and further into the surrounding bush, to collect pandanus and other wild fruit and nuts. She also went to the brackish water pools to collect water, which was as far away towards the mountain they had been until now.

# Chapter Five.
## Friends

Ekewane knew that on her old island there were different classes of people. She belonged to the *Ramaoide*, the elite members of the tribe. Then there were the *Enename*, the middle class who generally owned a great deal of land and had a high degree of influence over people; but could not make decisions in regard to the whole tribe. And lastly, there were the *Sitio.* These were 'slaves' or serf-life po*sitio*ns -people without land or prestige who worked the vegetable gardens for her parents and other high-ranking members. The *Sitio* were only allowed a small number of coconuts and pandanus from the trees belonging to the different families.

As a child she played with all the children in the village. As she became a little older, she could not remember when or why this had happened; her friends belonged to the two higher-level ranking classes.

Here on this new island she wondered if things would remain the same. She had always accepted the way things were back home, but now she wondered why. Ekewane did not ask her parents these questions, tribal laws or order were never questioned.

She had noticed a boy a little older than herself, always looking at her from a distance and often following her. He was only a few years older, but as he was tall and muscular, he looked much older. His name was Emarr, the same as her friend that had been on another canoe. She also noticed that the other members of her tribe treated this family differently.

Ekewane had made a new friend her own age. She had known Eiru on her old island, but never played or worked with her before because they both had other friends. Eiru was a little taller than her and very pretty. Eiru had two older siblings who were both married and remained behind on their island.

Ekewane and Eiru worked together helping the women. They collected shellfish, wove mats and baskets, scraped the coconut flesh to make milk and oil. They had learnt to catch the octopus from the holes on the reef by wriggling their fingers in the hole, and when the octopus grabbed hold, they would quickly pull it out. At first they were frightened and had difficulty in pulling them out at the right time, but slowly they improved and would often catch them. The girls quickly became good friends; they shared a small hut, and would lie awake late at night talking about their old island and the friends they left behind.

The girls had discovered a small niche cut into the limestone near the reef. The overhanging branches added to its attraction and seclusion; it had become their special place. At night before retiring to their hut, they would sit there watching the ever-changing sea. This was at the same time the other members of their tribe relaxed after their day's activities.

One night, as the girls sat watching the younger children play and the adults were sitting around the fire talking, Emarr was sitting away from everyone. He was always alone, Ekewane felt sorry for him and motioned him to join them. Eiru frowned but stayed quiet. Emarr came over and sat down quietly on the ground near them but did not speak.

Ekewane as usual started talking about her favorite topic; the mysterious dark mountain. She had become fascinated and drawn to the dark hovering silhouette, and often wondered what lived in the thick dark forest. Eiru as usual shuddered at the thought; they had often heard those frightening screams, and although Emanear reassured them that these spirits would not harm them, they were still afraid.

The two girls talked and Emarr sat there quietly listening. The moon was high in the sky and the cool breeze felt wonderful after the heat of the day. When they noticed that the adults were leaving their fires and going to sleep in the huts, the girls stood up and walked together to the hut they shared. Emarr also headed along the beach to where he slept.

That night, and many others that followed, Ekewane dreamt that she was walking through the forest. She was not afraid and felt happy and free to wander, just like she felt when she was home on her island. So one morning she made up her mind; she would go into the forest and climb only a little way up the mountain.

"Nobody will look for me during the day; everyone will be busy with different tasks . . . I will not ask Eiru, because she will be too scared . . . I will be back before the sun goes down, and if I bring back bird eggs or other food, my parents will be proud of me," she reasoned to herself.

But it was not easy to escape from Eiru. It was not until Eiru's mother called her that she made her escape. Ekewane had only walked a little distance when she heard footsteps running after her.

"Eiru go back!"

"No! I know where you are going, you can't go, it's dangerous," cried Eiru.

But Ekewane kept walking. "If you want to come, come, but don't go back and tell the tribe."

So the two girls set off through the dense undergrowth. Ekewane kept her axe close by, she felt braver holding it tight.

# Chapter Six.
## The Sinister Mountain

The two girls pushed and cut their way through the undergrowth. There was no sunlight above them; only thick dark green foliage surrounded them. Their bodies were full of scratches from the sharp hidden limestones and crevices they had to squeeze their way through. Some of these pinnacles towered so high the girls could not see the tops.

And still they walked on.

As the morning went on the girls had not come into any opening. Eiru had become more fearful every step, and was angry with herself for following Ekewane, but it was too late to find the way back herself. She sat down exhausted, there was no cool breeze like on the beach, the hot humid air made it difficult to breathe and she knew that she could not go on any further. So she put her head between her hands and cried: she wanted to be on the beach with her mother and the other members of the tribe.

After a few paces Ekewane became aware that she could not hear the moans and cries of Eiru, and slowly turned around to see why she was so quiet. Eiru was sitting further down the rough track. She quickly returned to her, afraid that she had been hurt. As she took the first step, the now familiar piercing scream rang out amongst the trees.

She froze. The screaming continued even louder, it was coming closer. Ekewane ran as fast as she could to where Eiru was sitting looking petrified and gazing up into the high trees: she had gone very pale. Ekewane sat down beside her friend and put her arms around her.

"I-it's all r-right,' she stammered, but did not look convinced. "M-my m-mother s-said that i-it w-will not h-harm us."

Eiru looked at her and whispered, "We have come into its land, it is angry with us, it will take us!"

Ekewane did not know how to comfort or convince her, because she knew that it was true. They had left the place where they would not be harmed and were now deep in the forest that belonged to this spirit.

The two girls sat there terrified waiting to be taken by the angry spirit. They listened attentively. They could hear the birds twittering high above them, and the breeze shuffling through the leaves on the high trees, but the loud piercing cry had become fainter and fainter.

For how long they sat their embracing they did not know, but their bodies ached from the tension. Ekewane slowly got up and spoke more confidently than she really felt.

"The spirit has gone, it understands that we mean it no harm."

"I want to go home," Eiru whispered still crying.

Ekewane nodded in agreement.  She did not feel as brave now, so they started back down the half hidden track they had just come from.

"I don't remember this place," Eiru whispered. She had been too afraid to speak since the terrifying scream.

"I think you are right, these trees don't look familiar," replied Ekewane not been able to disguise the fear in her voice.

They were lost and the tribe did not know they were even missing, and probably would not know for a long time. The children of the tribe ate and slept by themselves; the adults did not keep count of the older children.

The girls stopped and tried to see the sky above, but it was still hidden by the sickly green light that surrounded them. They had no water and were very thirsty, and knew that they would die; nobody could find them here. Each in their own thoughts felt sickened at the reality of their situation. Ekewane blamed herself for being so foolish.

"Maybe the spirit will come back and take us, it would be better than roaming aimlessly in this thick green foliage. Man eating tribes or savage animals could kill us," she thought.

She remembered how she felt on the canoe; the throbbing pain and cramps thirst and hunger had brought. The memory came rushing back and the tears began to swell in her eyes. Again she felt that nauseating fear.

They sat there for a long time not having the energy to keep walking. They did not know what to do or where to go, so they waited, for what they did not know, but they waited.

Nightfall came; they knew it was night because the dark green light became shadowy black. They could hear the strange noises that the night brings. The spirits have now left the underworld they thought, and would be here soon. They knew it would be useless to run, so they waited huddled together. But as the night continued the fatigue, fear and tension drifted away and they fell into a restless sleep.

They woke the next morning both looking around

surprised that they were still alive. Ekewane stood up and stretched, the forest did not look so dangerous this morning: they would find their way back. She smiled at Eiru to encourage her.

"Come on! We will find our way back home."

Eiru did not look as confident as her friend, but slowly got up and followed.

The girls started walking again not knowing in which direction they should go. They could not see the sun so they just kept walking.

They had only walked a little distance when Ekewane slipped. She screamed as she kept sliding down a steep hole that had been covered with dry branches.

She felt the rough terrain scrape away the skin from her body as she slid down faster and faster, and then a thump! All the air was crushed out of her lungs and she just lay there dazed. Only a few minutes had passed, but to Ekewane it felt a long time until her senses came back to her. She felt the air painfully flowing into her lungs again and heard Eiru's desperate screams from above.

Eiru screamed, and screamed, she could not stop. Then felt two strong, warm hands cover her mouth, and then everything went black and she dropped to the ground.

Emarr stood there looking down at Eiru. He knew she was unconscious, but did not know what to do, so left her lying there and walked carefully over to the edge, and looked down the steep incline. He could see Ekewane lying there, and felt a spasm of pain within his stomach, was she dead? He frantically called out her name, and slowly he could see her turning her head and look up at him in bewilderment.

"She is still alive!" he whispered.

"Where did Emarr come from?"

Ekewane could not make sense of what had happened and still felt stunned, so she slowly closed her eyes and went over her morning. She woke up with Eiru lying beside her, they got up and walked only a little way, then felt herself slipping down too fast for her to try and stop. She could feel the burning sensation where she had grazed her body whilst falling, but where did Emarr come from? And where was Eiru? For a long time she just looked dazed at the figure standing above the deep hole. Her breathing still felt painful and her body throbbed every time she tried to move.

## Chapter Seven.
## Emarr

Emarr sat alone on the warm sand, and watched the other children having fun diving under the waves that crashed onto the shore. He sat there silently knowing that he could never be that carefree; he was different.

His father, when he was younger, told him that he belonged to the *Sitio* - the serf class. His family was not allowed to own land or coconut trees, and often worked for the *Ramaoide* class. He had once asked why his family belonged to the *Sitio* class, and why they did not belong to the two upper classes.

His father had replied sadly: "It is the way of our people. In the past if we could prove our bravery, we would be given land, or coconut trees of our own, and then could become part of the *Ramaoide* class. But the times of valour and heroism have ended, and we must accept our place within the tribe."

Emarr was always conscious of this distinction between himself and other members of the village. There were others of the *Sitio* class, but he shunned away from everyone, not making friends with any of the boys his own age. At times the boys from the other two classes made fun of him. When he was younger he felt hurt at their cruelty, but as he grew older he ignored their sneers.

He was an only child. His small brothers and sister died when they were very young. He could still remember his little sister. He had often carried her on his back and played with her. He knew that his parents would rely on him in the future, but he did not mind. He felt angry and hated being made to feel inferior to those children now playing in the water. Emarr had one dream he kept to himself; he wanted to leave this island and take his parents to a better place, where they would be equal to the other villagers.

He often watched three friends play and knew their names. The small girl that seemed to be the leader was Ekewane, the great head chief's granddaughter. Her mother was also the most powerful sorceress in the village. The two young boys were Amweb and Emarr like himself, and they too belonged to the *Ramaoide* class.

He often thought that if his little sister was still alive she would be like the young slim girl, running free and having fun, not caring about classes and possessions.

The other girls her age living in the village never seemed to run around like her. Once they had finished their chores they would sit by their huts, combing and threading flowers in each other's hair, or weaving wreaths to wear on their heads. He had often heard them snigger as Ekewane walked past. But she did not seem to notice and lived in a world of adventure and fantasy, as she played with her friends.

He had already gone through puberty and his initiation ceremony. "I am now fourteen, and a man, and I will change things for my family!" he had thought.

At the time a special hut had been built for him and other boys that went through their initiation. Whilst he was living in this hut he was treated the same as the others. They stayed in this special hut for four weeks, ate special food that was prepared for them, and each day an elder member of the tribe would come and teach them wrestling, boxing and other sports. They were also taught many things about life, marriage and responsibilities. At the end of the four weeks there was a great ceremony. He was aware that his parents could not provide the same elaborate celebration as some of the other boys, but he did not care, in his eyes and the eyes of the villagers he had become a man, and his parents were very proud of him.

"I will change my future!" he promised himself as he watched the slim girl walk towards him. She was about eleven; her long black hair wet from the seawater, and her bright brown eyes sparkled with mischief. She glanced at him sitting there, but did not give any sign of recognition and started running along the beach.

Emarr was tall and muscular. Because he was taller than the other boys of his age, he looked older and he felt proud of this fact. His black hair reached his shoulders like the other men of the village, but he never let it loose like the others -it annoyed him, so he tied it behind his head.

He had heard that some of the villagers would leave the island and wanted to be part of this group. However, he knew his father had no say in the matter and he had no power to speak. One morning when he left his hut that he shared with other boys of his age, he went to see his parents.

"Emarr, we too shall leave this island with the other families," his father had said.

Emarr could not believe it! He thought he must have misunderstood, and slowly looked at his mother and she nodded. He felt and exhilarating current of joy sweep through him and wanted to scream out; they would finally leave this island his dream had come true.

The following months he was part of the teams of men preparing the canoes. He felt wonderful being part of this adventure. "Anywhere will be better than here!" he kept thinking to himself.

The journey across the sea had been difficult. It took a long time and there was barely enough food or water to survive - but they did.

The canoes in the great sea separated, and they could no longer see any of the villagers that had left with them. Emarr knew that Ekewane and her family had also left the island; he did not know why but was happy that she would be there in their new home.

When the storms came the others thought that they would all drown: he knew they would survive. From time to time he wondered what had become of chief Erangue and hoped they too had survived; it saddened him to think that the little courageous girl would be lost at sea.

And then the day came when they saw the island. The families in the canoe were happy, land at last! Yet they were afraid of what they would find on the island, but again he knew they would survive.

When they were closer to the island they could see

people running and waving their arms happy to see them. The people ran out to greet them and when they were close to the reef, helped them pull their canoe ashore. Once on shore they were offered food and water.

He had sat down on the sand exhausted and only looked up when two small hands put a coconut under his nose. He lifted his eyes only to look into two large brown mischievous eyes. He blinked and felt stunned, "Ekewane?" he asked, the girl looked at him, smiled, and then skipped away.

The days that followed were exciting. They travelled north along the shore looking for other members of their village. Although people were still afraid of what the island held, everyone was grateful to be on land.

Emarr always kept Ekewane in his sight. He felt uneasy about what could lay ahead of them, so he always stayed nearby in case of danger. He did not understand why, but felt protective of the young girl and did not want any harm to come to her. He had turned fifteen on the boat coming over, but no one acknowledged this date, as they were overwhelmed with the difficulties and danger that every day brought.

It was one night many weeks after their arrival and

they had finally returned to their first camp, that Emarr was as usual sitting not far from where Ekewane and her friend Eiru always sat, when Ekewane called him over. He was shocked but went over and sat down on the ground nearer to them. He felt awkward and embarrassed, so he did not speak. He sat there happy to listen to their chatter. Emarr could hear Ekewane's excitement when she talked about the mountain; surely he thought she is only dreaming about it.

He would often lay awake at night listening to the horrible screaming coming from the mountain. He knew it was the spirit world, and that Ekewane's mother had assured them that the spirits would not harm them, but he still felt the hair behind his neck tingle every time he heard that piercing scream; the mountain is warning us not to go there he thought, it is the land of the spirits and we do not belong.

That night listening to Ekewane talking excitedly about the mountain, a strange suspicion came over him; he did not trust her.

He awoke with an uneasy feeling; there had been something in Ekewane's behaviour the night before that made him suspicious. It was still morning when he noticed her creeping away into the undergrowth and decided to follow at a distance.

"I will only come out if she needs me. Perhaps she is only going to fetch water.

He had been hiding, when he heard Eiru running after her. He stopped and watched the girls arguing, and then they both continued walking.

"She will not go far, because of her young friend. I'll wait near the ponds until they return."

He sat down near the water deep in his thoughts. The peaceful water and the heat of the day made him drowsy and fell asleep. He woke up startled, the screaming from the mountain had awoken him, and it sounded much louder and terrifying.

"The spirit of the mountain is angry!"

"Ekewane, Eiru?" he whispered.

He did not think they had returned because he would have heard them talking and laughing as they usually did when they were together. He quickly got up and looked at the track where the girls had gone and felt undecided.

"Maybe I am being foolish and overprotective . . . but I will follow their path for a little way ahead."

At one point he thought he heard screams, but was not sure, they were a long way away and could have been the spirits from the mountain. It was becoming dark he could feel the undergrowth become cooler as the sun was setting.

Emarr knew that it was useless trying to follow the girls in the dark. "I am foolish as the girls are probably back at camp, they may have returned another way."

He was unsure what to do, but finally decided that he would sleep there for the night. He looked at the surrounding trees and saw that there were tall coconut trees nearby, so climbed up and cut some coconuts down.

He did not sleep well that night; afraid for himself and the uncertainty of the two girls. As soon as the first rays of light filtered through the trees, he looked around again to see if he could see any of the branches cut or broken by the girls.

He sighed seeing their track. He wanted to return to the village so he could go fishing, so he hurried. He thought that if the girls had returned, their track would soon go back down towards the sea. But instead it kept climbing up the side of the mountain.

"They did not return they must be still on the

mountain. If I hurry the girls may be still asleep somewhere not too far ahead," he reasoned out aloud.

And then he heard it, not the piercing screams of the spirits.

"EKEWANE!" he yelled.

He did not breathe and remained rooted to the forest floor, too shocked to move.

Then he heard more screams! They were panic-stricken. He could tell that the girl screaming had lost all control and given way to fear.

So he ran, and ran, slipping on the branches that lay hidden across his path.

He felt the sting of deep scratches on his arms and legs as he ran as fast as he could. The screams were getting louder and louder. "Just a little way ahead!" he told himself, and he prayed silently to his ancestors.

He came to a small clearing, and saw Eiru standing over what seemed a large crevice in the ground, she had her hands stretched out in front of her and was screaming hysterically.

"NO!" he yelled, and ran up to Eiru.

He put his hands on her shoulders, but she was oblivious to him and would not stop screaming, so gently placed his hand over her mouth to make her stop, but as soon as his hand felt her warm breath, she collapsed.

He looked at Eiru only for a moment and then down at where she had been gazing. Ekewane was lying at the bottom of a deep hole. The hole was steep, and at the bottom it was the size of two large huts.

"EKEWANE! EKEWANE!" he shouted. And then relief flowed through him, and he felt the air flow out of his lungs; he had not breathed since he heard those awful screams. Ekewane turned her head and looked at him bewildered.

"Ekewane!" Emarr called out again.

"I'm - all - right . . . but . . . the hole is too steep . . . I cannot climb up."

He could barely make out what she had said, her voice was rasping, as if she was in pain.

# Chapter Eight.

## The Appearance

Emarr turned quickly and left. With the disappearance of Emarr she felt abandoned.

"Eiru has probably fallen down another hole, and is dead," she thought to herself. And with that thought she felt even more wretched, it was her fault, Eiru did not want to come, but she was her friend and did not want her to go alone.

She fought back the tears. Her body was aching and the skin that had been scraped off, burnt. She kept her eyes fixed on the opening above her head, hoping to see one of her friends soon, before she gave way to the tears that were welling up inside her. And then finally Eiru peeked over the edge. Ekewane felt so grateful that she was still alive, now she thought if she were to die, at least Eiru was safe.

Then she saw Emarr standing beside her friend and was concentrating very hard. She could make out the expression in his face. Then he threw down a vine; but it did not reach the bottom.

"I'll try to climb a little way up, and maybe reach the

vine," she reasoned courageously.

She painfully stood up and looked at the steep embankment. The scratches burned, and her body was already showing the dark marks of her bruises. "At least I have not broken any bones." She tried to climb but kept slipping, it was too steep and was unable to find a footing on the sides.

"I can't climb up that high!"

Emarr looked down and then turned to Eiru, said something that Ekewane could not hear, then disappeared again. She knew that he would come back for her, so she sat down on the ground again and waited.

Emarr returned before very long, this time holding onto a trunk of an old coconut tree.

"Move as far away as you can from the edge!" he called down.

So she went to the other side of the hole and leaned against the side. Emarr pulled up the vine, tied it around the trunk and carefully lowered it down the hole. Once it had almost reached the bottom, he gave a sharp tug and the trunk dislodged itself from the vine. Ekewane looked incredulous, how did he do that?

"Put the trunk against the side and climb up to the

vine!" shouted Emarr.

She tried a few times, but kept slipping off the trunk that was covered in a slippery green moss, the more times she failed the more she felt frustrated and each time adding to the already badly bruised body.

"Take your time, go slow!" called down Emarr.

So she tried again. After a few more attempts she started to slowly climb further up.

"I have to put one foot up, then test it, then lift up the other foot, test it and continue this way until I reach the top of the log," she kept telling herself. But when she had reached the end of the precarious trunk, she still could not reach the vine.

"Now, try and balance yourself on your feet, so you can free your hands!" called down Emarr.

At first she felt afraid that if she let her hands go she would slip again. She looked up at Emarr and could see that he was smiling encouraging her and felt more confident, so she slowly let go and reached as high as she could. She closed her eyes anticipating the fall instead felt the vine in her hands and grasped it with all her strength, as her feet lost their balance. She knew her arms would not hold her for long as she dangled on the vine; she was not that strong.

"Hold on!" yelled Emarr and with this last encouragement she felt herself been hoisted up, using her feet against the sides she tried to climb and balance herself.

She looked up and saw Emarr and Eiru's faces strained as they pulled and pulled. She could see them come closer and closer; her eyes locked onto Emarr, and felt the strength flowing within him. One last pull and she felt her body coming over the edge.

The three of them sat down exhausted.

They sat there for some time without speaking, and then Emarr stood up.

He gathered some dry grass and small sticks, and then took out two saltwater-bush sticks from the pouch around his waist. He put the larger of the two sticks on the ground; it had a small hole in the middle. Then placed the smaller stick in the hole and started rubbing it faster and faster. Soon smoke could be seen from the dry leaves under the sticks. He carefully blew onto the leaves and small flames appeared.

"Stay here," he said and slowly walked into the dense forest.

The girls sat there and watched him disappear into the undergrowth. Although it was very hot the fire felt reassuring.

Ekewane had not noticed before, but they were in a small clearing. She could see patches of blue sky through the tall trees, and the black noddy birds flying above. Seeing the sun made the girls feel better, they had spent a day surrounded by the shadowy green light of leaves from the tall trees and thick bushes. They felt hot and exhausted so lay down to wait for Emarr.

They had fallen asleep and were awakened by the mouth-watering smell of meat cooking. They sat up and looked around confused. The sizzling sound and delicious smell was coming from the fire.

Emarr had three noddy birds speared through the middle with a stick. He was slowly turning them over the fire. The girls had not eaten since they had left their camp and the smell was intoxicating. Emarr did not look at them, he knew they were awake and watching him, so he slowly nodded towards a small pile of coconuts by his side. The girls quickly went over and picked up one each. They pierced the holes and drank thirstily; once they had finished they quickly picked up a second.

Ekewane thought she could see Emarr smile, it was the first time she had seen him smile. She picked up her empty coconuts found a sharp rock and expertly broke the coconut in half, then got a stick and scraped the soft flesh from the nut, but instead of eating it, handed it to Emarr. He was taken aback by her gesture, but quickly took the coconut flesh from her, and embarrassed continued concentrating on the roasting birds.

Eiru had also scooped out the sweet flesh and was eating it; she was so hungry and did not notice Ekewane's gesture. Their thirst quenched, the two girls sat beside Emarr and watched the fire flicker.

Ekewane was staring at the flickering flames when she saw the strange image of a man. The image was translucent, but she could make out his strange pale yellow skin, short straight black hair and strange brown almond shaped eyes. His body was clothed in a delicately woven material. He did not say anything, just smiled at her; there was something vaguely familiar about this spirit image, but she had never seen such a strange man before, so could not understand this familiar sensation. Then the image disappeared just as quickly as it came.

Ekewane became aware that Emarr and Eiru were

gazing at her. "Had they also seen the strange man-spirit in the fire?" she thought.

"Ekewane are you all right?" asked Eiru's soft voice.

"Why?"

"You were looking into the fire and started chanting like your mother," replied the frightened Eiru.

Ekewane looked at Emarr he was also gazing at her.

"I don't know," she replied and did not tell them what she had seen; she did not understand herself, so how could she explain this strange apparition.

Emarr pulled the noddy birds from the stick, and handed them to girls. He then did the same with the other small bird and began to eat. The meat was hot and delicious, they had not eaten meat since before they left their island home, and it felt strange and wonderful in their mouths.

"How did you catch the birds?" asked Eiru.

Emarr pulled out from his pouch a long twisted string that had a stone tied to the end. The girls had seen the men of their village catch birds that way, they would throw the tied stone into the air and if they were skilful enough, the stone would wrap around the flying bird's legs, and then they would pull it down. It took a lot of ability and practice to catch birds this way, and the girls were impressed the second time today by Emarr's skills.

High in the sky a frigate bird circled and cried out. They looked at each other frightened.

"This way," Ekewane said getting up and started walking determinately into the undergrowth again. The other two followed without asking questions.

Ekewane had lost her axe, so they took longer to make their way through the tangled vines and bushes. They smelt the flowers of the tomano trees, but could only see their large trunks, the top branches towered high above the canopy, and still they kept walking. They noticed that they were walking slightly downhill and the trees became sparser. Every now and again they came across a small clearing and the rays of the sun would shine down on them.

Then all of a sudden, they stopped. They could hear the sound of water! but it was not the sound of waves but soft and flowing. The men from their tribe had not come this far, so they continued to walk cautiously – aware that there could be another tribe living there.

They eventually came out onto a larger clearing and

there in front of them was a sheet of shimmering water. It was much larger than the brackish pools found around the island. This was very big. Emarr walked ahead of the girls and looked around carefully, he could not see any signs of danger so he motioned them to follow him. He went to the side of the lake, knelt down, dipped his cupped hands into the water and tasted it.

"Drink," he smiled. It was the second time they had seen him smile.

The two girls imitated him; the water was sweet, almost like the water from their village. It tasted sweeter than the water they had found in the pools along the beach.

After drinking their fill, they splashed their bodies with the cool clear water, it felt wonderful and refreshing, and although it burnt where the bushes had scratched them, they felt invigorated. Satisfied they sat down, happier than they had been in the past two days.

Emarr looked at the sky and said, "We need to build a hut, it will rain tonight."

They gathered the branches and leaves around the lake. He then put them expertly together and when they had finished he looked satisfied.

The girls were happy that only one hut was built,

because they were secretly afraid of sleeping alone; Emarr's presence made them feel safe.

Emarr climbed the tall coconut tree nearby and cut down some coconuts and fresh leaves. The leaves would be laid on the ground inside their hut and make soft beds for the night.

"I will be back soon," he said, when he climbed down.

The girls lay the leaves inside their hut and waited. Not long after he had left Emarr returned holding his arms full of mangoes. He had spotted the tall trees when he was cutting down the coconuts. The girls jumped up and ran happily towards him, this would be a feast! Sweet mangoes. Emarr laid the fruit carefully down and then left again towards the lake.

They watched him as he sharpened the end of a long stick with his stone knife, and then looked into the water. He concentrated for only a few minutes, and then threw the spear. He gave a cry of joy and pulled up a large milkfish. The girls could not believe it! Milkfish was a rare delicacy in their village.

Ekewane thought maybe they had died and this was the after-world.

"Isn't he wonderful," whispered Eiru.

Ekewane looked at Emarr and felt an overpowering feeling stir deep within her. For a moment she sat silently trying to understand this sensation. It somehow frightened her to go any further trying to understand, so she just shuddered and erased it from her mind.

# Chapter Nine.
## The Hidden Lake

*Inland brackish-water lake*

All night the rain poured down. The noise was so deafening that they could not sleep. At one stage the hut started to sway with the force of the wind, and they thought that they would be blown away.

Ekewane and Eiru huddled together afraid of the loud noises the wind and rain were making. There had been bad storms on their island, but they could not remember them this bad. So the three lay there awake, listening. Ekewane did not know why, it may have been the memory of her mother in times of danger, and without realising she started chanting the same song as her mother often did. Eiru and Emarr lay there listening to the soothing notes and they too felt braver.

The sun was high in the sky when they awoke. The storm had passed and they had fallen asleep during the long night. The sun felt familiar on their skin as they ate the night's leftovers. Ekewane and Eiru then walked towards the lake and followed it around until they came to a small inlet. They then took off their grass skirts and glided into the water. They bathed in the beautiful clear water; it was the first time since they had left their island that they were able to bathe in fresh sweet water instead of the seawater.

The girls felt happy and free as they swam and splashed around.

After a while they got out.  Since they landed on the island their skins had returned to a beautiful golden bronze, they had lost that sallow orange tinge the long months at sea had caused. Their long black wavy hair glittered, as the sun caught the drops of water, as they ran their fingers through it.

As they reached their makeshift camp, Emarr was sitting there smiling. He too had bathed in the lake. As they sat down beside him he shyly took two frangipanis from behind his back and handed them to the two girls. The two girls happily placed them in their hair.

"I wish we could stay here," Emarr said wistfully.

"We can't, our families will worry about us, but we will come back again," smiled Ekewane.

She slowly got up first and the other two followed. They looked around one more time and started walking towards the undergrowth. The descent was steep and they would often slipped on the wet ground.

It was only later on that day when they sat down hot and tired, that they listened attentively. In the distance they could hear the sound of the waves crashing against the shore. They looked at each other, soon they would reach the sea and then they would follow the coast until they found their families.

They got up excitedly, forgetting how tired and hot they were and hurried as fast as the bushes would allow them. Ekewane noticed that as they came closer to the sea, Emarr was becoming more somber, and wondered why?

"Oh!" screamed Eiru.

She had not seen the large rock and fell over it. Ekewane walked back to help her up, but she stopped and looked alarmed.

"Emarr!" she shouted.

Emarr ran back as fast as he could. Ekewane pointed to what at first sight looked like one of the many large rocks.

"I-it's not a r-rock, i-it's a large bone," she stuttered.

Emarr examined the rock carefully. "You are right, but I have never seen such a big bone, I don't know what it belongs to." He looked worried, what sort of monsters lived on this island?

Eiru still on the ground started to cry again. She was exhausted and afraid yet again.

"We will keep going, the sea is getting closer, and don't be afraid Eiru." Emarr declared more courageously than he felt.

So the three continued walking. They did not dare speak, and would often glance around looking for any animal that could come out from behind a tree, or pinnacle, and attack them.

The sound of the ocean became louder and louder until they finally stepped out of the forest, and there, in front of them, was the great expansion of blue. They gazed up and down the reef in order to see if their tribe was anywhere near, but could see only the deserted shoreline. They did not know where they were, but felt safer, and would follow the reef until they found their tribe.

The three walked all morning. When the sun was high in the sky, Emarr looked at the high coconut trees close to the shore.

"I will get some coconuts for us." He then walked towards the tree and the girls followed.

They watched him skillfully climb a tall tree and cut the coconuts, balancing only on his feet as he reached up above his head. Once he had thrown down a few, he slowly climbed down.

The girls found a sharp limestone pinnacle and cut the thick husk. They handed the first coconut to Emarr and smiled, then set about opening their own. They drank the sweet coconut water and then proceeded to scrape out the soft flesh. They were not in any hurry, the day was hot and they were tired so lay back under the shade and rested.

A cool breeze woke them up. They felt better after their short sleep and were now ready to continue their walk. The three friends kept walking silently each in their own thoughts, until in the distance they could see a large group of people spread along the shoreline. They knew that finally they had found their tribe.

Ekewane was concerned that her parents and other adults would have now become aware of their disappearance and be very angry. It was her fault that Eiru and Emarr had left the encampment, so they would be angrier at her than the other two. She sighed and prepared herself.

She knew she would not be physically punished, because children were never punished that way, but be made to stay on the reef, and not even be allowed to go fetch the water only a short distance away.

As they came closer, the children ran towards them excitedly. The adults also noticed them. Ekewane could distinguish the tall figure amongst the other adults; it was her father.

## Chapter 10
## The Tribes

The group quickly surrounded the three and even the children were silent. Ekewane could feel her heart pounding in her chest; she had still held out the slight hope that the adults had not missed them. When they were back on their island, she would stay with friends and other relatives and sometimes not see her parents for days, but here things might now be different.

"Where have you been?" asked angrily her father.

"We went to fetch water, and walked a little further than we thought, and got lost," she explained.

She did not think telling the truth would be the best solution at this time.

"All of you together to fetch water?" he asked, eyeing Emarr suspiciously.

"No, Eiru and I went, and Emarr noticed we were missing and followed our tracks in case we got lost," she replied sincerely, because this part was the truth.

"You have been gone three nights, where did you go?" he continued questioning.

Ekewane looked at Eiru and Emarr they both stood there silently looking at the ground. Ekewane felt anger rising, they had returned safe didn't they? The adults shouldn't make her friends feel so guilty, it was her fault, they only wanted to help her in case she got into some problems, which she did of course, she thought, but these details she would never tell.

"We found a large beautiful, sweet water lake, full of milk fish and surrounded by mango trees," she said triumphantly, hoping that this news would lessen the adults' anger.

It seemed to work! The members of the tribe started whispering excitedly amongst themselves.

Erangue looked gravely at her and weighed up this last piece of information, then turned to the rest of the tribe and said, "We will find out more information about this lake later tonight, now we must continue to fish."

It worked! Ekewane thought thankfully, even though she knew she had not yet been excused, but the worst was over.

Emanear then embraced her. Eiru's mother also embraced her daughter and looked relieved, she had noticed her missing and was worried. Ekewane looked around to see where Emarr was, and saw him walking silently away with his father and she wondered where his mother was, but did not have time to think any more of Emarr, because her mother was speaking to her and she returned her attention to what she was saying.

"You will come with me to collect the plants we need for our medicine," and handed her a basket woven from the coconut leaves, and although Ekewane felt very tired she did not argue. She knew that her mother was teaching her the secrets and magic that had been handed down from her grandmother, and her mother before, since time began. She wanted to learn, because she knew that one day, like her mother, people would come to her for help. She remembered the strange spirit seen in the fire, and wondered if she should ask her mother about it, but decided not tell anyone.

Late that night the three sat in their familiar spot on the shoreline, not speaking just looking at the other children play. Emarr was sitting on the ground a little distance from them looking preoccupied.

Two girls sat only a short distance away from them playing 'string figures'. The string was made of plaited human hair. Some figures were made using four or five loops, but some figures were more complicated and 23 handspans of string was used. Each girl looped the string between her fingers making complex patterns. The girls took it in turns and chanted a story whilst using the figures to illustrate their story.

Groups of boys were engrossed playing marbles with the tomano nuts. It looked very peaceful, but Ekewane knew she would be called to speak again to the tribal adults and she felt guarded.

The two girls stopped their game and walked over to Ekewane and Eiru.

"You think you are better than all of us don't you?" sniggered the prettier of the two girls. The other girl just giggled.

Ekewane knew their names they were Emet and Iud.  Emet was very pretty, her long black wavy hair reach down below her waist, and her skin was a beautiful smooth gold. Ekewane often watched Emet and thought her vain. She was the daughter of Ramanmada, another head of the elite *Ramaoide* class. Ekewane knew that one day their new island would be divided. Emet would eventually inherit her mother's land, as was the custom in their tribe. The women of the tribe would own the land

and coconut trees, although the men would leave their weapons, canoes and tools to their sons. The land would usually be passed down from mother to daughter; the oldest daughter inheriting the larger portion of their land. Emet would become very wealthy, and she knew that many young men of the village wanted to marry her.

Iud was the taller of the two girls. She was not as pretty or graceful as Emet, but followed her around looking as if she were grateful for Emet's friendship.

Ekewane looked at Emet shocked, not understanding what she had meant.

"You are like your father always thinking you are above everyone else. The rest of the tribe thinks you are just a silly girl!" With that they walked away laughing.

Ekewane felt her eyes swell with tears. She did not understand. Eiru held her hand and said nothing. Emarr nearby noticed the encounter and silently got up and sat next to her without saying a word. Ekewane felt better with Eiru and Emarr by her side; they were her friends. But she did not understand why the two girls disliked her; she had done nothing to offend them.

She did not have time to dwell on the unpleasant encounter, because she could see one of the adults,

Dobague, walking towards them. Ekewane felt her heart thump, and knew they had been summoned. The three friends got up and slowly walked back with him.

When they arrived to where the adults of the tribe were sitting around a large fire, they sat down. Ekewane looked at her friends, they looked just as fearful as she was, so she concentrated on the fire in the middle and not look at anyone.

"Tell us about what you saw in the mountain?" said a man's voice.

Ekewane opened her mouth, but could not speak; Emarr having become aware of her apprehension started explaining.

She could hear his voice as from a distance tell the elders about the dense forest, high pinnacles, but she noticed that he too did not say anything about the incident of her falling into the deep hole. Emarr then went on explaining about the lake. His voice was becoming fainter and fainter, a murmur in her head.

She kept her eyes fixed on the flickering flames, and then without warning the red flames turned into blood, she could not look away and watched horrified.

Her vision seemed to zoom out from the patch of

blood and saw many of her people lying on the ground all with the same sickly red blood oozing from wounds on their bodies. She looked more carefully and saw that spears and other weapons caused the wounds. Her vision desperately searched the scene to see if she could see any of her family and friends, her heart was now beating faster and faster she could not stop the loud pounding in her ears.

Ekewane felt her body being lightly shaken. Even before she awoke, for she felt she had fallen into a deep trance as she had seen some of the other sorceresses of their village, and felt afraid, because she had had no control over her body or the spirit world. She heard her mother's comforting voice from a distance.

"Ekewane, wake up," crooned her mother. Ekewane slowly opened her dazed eyes and felt confused.

Her mother helped her sit up whilst Ekewane looked around frightened. The images from her nightmare were still vivid in her mind.

"Ekewane did you see something in the flames?" asked her mother.

Ekewane did not answer but looked at her startled, had her mother also seen those terrible scenes?

"You mustn't worry, they are the images the spirit world have sent to you. Have you seen them before?"

Ekewane hesitated for a few minutes until she could formulate the word in her mind, "Yes," she whispered.

"Did you see images in the fire?" Her mother looked at her intently and Ekewane felt uncomfortable.

"You have strong magic in your blood, it comes from my mother, her mother and all mothers before them. I cannot see images, but I know when something will happen, whether it is a good or evil spirit. My grandmother often told me about her mother, she too could see the pictures like you. They are of what will come. You have inherited more powerful magic than me." Then she smiled. "Don't be afraid of the spirit world, they are not your enemies." And with that she hugged her and walked away.

Ekewane looked around still confused and fearful. She was sitting inside her hut and wondered how she got there. She was trying to re-live her last memory when Eiru put her head inside the hut.

"Are you all right?"

Ekewane nodded and then Eiru disappeared. She could hear her whispering in the nearby bushes, and then silently came back and lay beside her.

"Emarr was worried." And with that she turned over on her side and went to sleep. She did not ask Ekewane about the strange occurrence, she would tell her when she was ready, Eiru thought as she drifted off to sleep.

Ekewane lay down again, and the tears ran down her face. She was not frightened anymore at what she had seen, but she knew that a lot of suffering was ahead for her and her people.

# Chapter Eleven.
## Strangers arrive on Volcanic Island

*Arrival of other islanders.*

The tribe was awakened by loud shouts. Ekewane and Eiru quickly sat up.

"Strangers!" cried a voice from the reef.

Ekewane's vision came back to her. The memory of the blood made her feel sick, but she quickly jumped up and ran down to the edge of the reef and stopped.

Out on the horizon there was a large canoe; she knew it was not from her village because the outrigger was on the left hand side.

"These strangers will kill my people!" she thought horrified. She did not see Eiru or Emarr, but felt their presence beside her and felt a little more courageous.

Ekewane looked at the men of her tribe, they were all armed and standing in front of the women and children. She noticed her father, and yet again he was wearing the prestigious armband. She also glimpsed quickly at Emarr, he stood close to her looking grave and clutching his spear tightly.

Nobody spoke, not even the smaller children that never seemed to stop making noises, they were holding tightly onto their mothers.

The large canoe came closer and closer to the reef. Ekewane could see that there were women and children on board. Everyone watched and waited silently. She could imagine the fear of the people on board, just as they felt only a short time before when they had arrived on this island.

Without thinking she left her friends' side, and walked slowly towards the men still standing on at the edge of the reef, watching intently the advancing canoe. Eiru although afraid, walked slowly behind her, and Emarr never left her side.

When she reached her mother who was standing just behind her father. Her mother turned around, looked at her and nodded. Then she whispered something in her father's ear.

"They will not harm us!" shouted her father.

The tribe looked at him. Ekewane heard an angry murmur from some of the men, but they did not voice their displeasure.

The people in the canoe were waving anxiously. And then suddenly she waved back, Eiru and Emarr followed her example, soon most of the tribe doing the same. They did not want to irritate the occupants of the canoe - if they had come in peace?

The strangers had come from another island and were welcomed. Many canoes had left the islands because of the long years of drought, just as Ekewane's tribe had this canoe also lost sight of the others soon after they left.

The strangers settled into the larger established group. The children quickly made friends with the children already on the island, and the adults shared their food, very soon they became part of the tribe.

On the second day after their arrival, a boy came up to them. He was the same age as Emarr, and had the same strong muscular build but was a little taller.

Bagonoun was not as grave as Emarr, he laughed at many of the things the girls said, and seemed to be always happy. The three did not mind him joining their small group. At night he would often talk about the humorous things he did back when he was on his island and their friendship became stronger.

The expedition to the lake organized by the elders was temporarily postponed. Ekewane and her friends often talked about their mystical lake, and Bagonoun was excited at the prospect of visiting this wonderful place.

# Chapter Twelve.
## Return to the Lake.

One morning not long after the arrival of the canoe, Emanear came to them and said; "Get ready you are leaving with some of the men."

The girls understood what Emanear meant. They looked at each other and walked slowly to the group of men standing together talking. They were carrying their weapons. Ekewane looked quickly around to see where Emarr was. He stood a little apart from the group and nodded to her, Bagonoun stood near him excited and anxious to leave. Ekewane wondered why the men let the girls come along, but did not ask.

Her father seemed to give some unspoken signal to move. She felt tension amongst the men, but nobody spoke out, and the small group started walking back around the coastline, from where she and her friends had come from some weeks before.

The small group continued walking for most of the day. It was late in the afternoon when Emarr pointed to the men where they had come out from the undergrowth. The men decided to stop there the night and continue next morning. The sky was clear so they did not expect it to rain that night.

Some of the men went to the edge of the reef and dived in. They soon came back up holding different kinds of fish; the reef around the entire island was rich with fish. Other men climbed up the tall coconut trees and cut down coconuts.

Ekewane and Eiru gathered leaves from the surrounding bushes and laid them on the ground; they would sleep on the soft fresh leaves. They then went along the reef collecting periwinkles and other shellfish. Once they had gathered sufficient they returned to where the men had lit a fire, and put some of the dried coconut leaves on the ground nearby, then placed the shells on top, and covered them with another layer of leaves and set it alight.

The girls watched the flames leaping high into the sky. Ekewane turned away quickly; she had become afraid of looking into the flames. So while Eiru sat waiting for the flames to go out, she went into the nearby undergrowth where she had seen smaller coconut trees, cut a long stem and carried it back. She sat down and slit the stem in half, she then gave half to Eiru and the other half she kept herself. The girls then wove the leaves to form moon shaped plates.

It was still daylight and they watched Emarr and Bagonoun come out of the water, both boys were holding two large eels. They walked over to the girls, cut the eels into pieces and placed them in one of the large coconut leaf plates. The girls ate the raw eel with relish, they had not eaten since they had left that morning, and were hungry.

Other men were now also sitting around the fire eating fish and drinking coconut water. Ekewane picked out some of the shellfish from the ashes and placed them in the other coconut leaf plate, together with a hand full of small sticks, which would be used to pick out the flesh from the shells, carried them over to her father.

Ekewane's father was as usual at the centre of the group; he looked over at her and smiled to reassure her. The island still held many mysteries, so people were still preoccupied with imminent dangers that could be around.

Ekewane did not feel afraid, she looked at the men of her tribe and her eyes fell on Emarr talking amongst them; no, she thought, I am not in danger.

Emarr sensed her gaze and quickly glanced at her

whilst continuing explaining to the men about the route they would be taking.

Bagonoun happily left the men and came to sit beside the girls. He and Eiru started talking and laughing together.

Ekewane sat silently, and although she did not want to look into the flames, the flickering kept drawing her attention until they held her prisoner.

She heard her heart beat faster and faster, as she became more and more terrified of those magnetic flames. Then as before, a haze started forming within the flames. The haze swirled around until the image of a man appeared and looked at her from the flames. This time however, he was white like the clouds in the sky, his eyes were pieces of sky and his hair was golden like the sand of their island. He wore a fine weave that covered his body; it too was white. The man looked at her sadly, she gazed at him and thought once again how familiar he looked. But then he turned away and slowly disintegrated into the flames.

For a moment she felt sad, the spirit had smiled and then left her feeling empty. She could not understand why these spirits were so different and yet so familiar. She became aware of a hand gently squeezing hers, and the flames let her go.

Emarr was now sitting beside her looking at her. Eiru and Bagonoun were still laughing at something he had said, the men were still engrossed in their conversations, and she felt relieved that nobody besides Emarr had noticed her strange withdrawal from the world around her.

The following morning the small group headed up the mountain towards the lake. Emarr was in front with Bagonoun, and the girls were at the back.

Ekewane could not remember any of the trees along the way, as they all looked the same. Later on that morning she did notice that the trees were becoming taller and taller, and the undergrowth was not as impenetrable.

They did not stop until they had come to the tall mango trees. The trees were very big and on the ground there were many ripe mangoes, fallen from the branches high above them.

The small group stopped and ate the sweet juicy fruit. When they were all satisfied they happily stood up and continued to follow Emarr.

Only a little way further they could hear the wind blowing through the canopy above them and the faint sound of water splashing against the limestone pinnacles that surrounded the lake. Everyone started walking faster. They stopped in unison in front of the large lake, too surprised to speak. Then the men started talking all at once. Ekewane could not understand what they were saying, everyone was excited!

They walked to the edge of the lake and, as Ekewane and her friends had done a few weeks earlier, cupped their hands and drank the sweet water.

The men were excited as they could see the large milkfish swimming in the lake. It was the largest fresh water supply they had seen so far on the island. Now they knew that even in times of drought they would have water.

The girls walked over to Emarr and Bagonoun, and Ekewane asked: "Did you tell the men about the large bone we found?"

"I did but I couldn't find it again to show them," replied Emarr seriously.

Ekewane and Eiru looked at each other and walked away from the men. They wanted to bathe again in the cool clear water and started walking away from the group.

The girls walked further around the lake. They could still hear the men's excited voices; they were catching milkfish to take back to the main camp. They walked around a small bend; the branches of trees were hanging over the water. Eiru was the first to take off her grass skirt and was happily entering the water.

"NO!" Ekewane yelled.

Eiru froze and looked startled. She quickly turned around at Ekewane.

"W-what?"

"You must not go in there, look! The water is not smooth like the rest of the lake. It is swirling and it is breathing! Look Eiru, look how black it is!"

Eiru screamed and jumped out of the water.

"Do you think that large bone was from the animal that lives in this deep hole?" she asked frightened.

"I don't know, but that hole is dangerous I can feel it . . . an evil spirit lives in there."

The two girls walked back closer to where the men were fishing and bathed at the edge of the lake. They then sat down near where some of the men were fishing and Ekewane again cut some of stems from the nearby small coconut trees. The girls wove two large baskets; they would carry back mangoes for the members of the tribe that stayed behind.

The men did not take very long to catch many large milkfish. They threaded them through long sticks so that two men on either side could carry them.

"We will leave now," said Erangue

"Who gives you always the right to make decisions?" replied the angry voice from one of the men. It was Ramanmada.

" I am the head chief on this island!" replied angrily Erangue.

"There has not been a vote to see who will be the head chief. Just because you have the armband, and your father was the head chief. Your family does not have the power here as you did back on our old island!" Ramanmada yelled back angrily.

"You are right, but until we do vote, I was the first to land, and I DO have the armband. We will leave now so we can return to our camp before the fish cannot be eaten. They will rot in this heat. If we go down this mountain before dark we can follow the shoreline until we reach our camp. We will be home tonight. I am leaving now if you want to remain; stay, Ekewane, Eiru, Emarr, come. "

Ekewane got up, followed by Eiru. Emarr, Bagonoun and his father also stood up to leave. The remaining two men did not want to remain there alone, so they followed Erangue and his group.

Soon they came to the mango trees. Eiru and Ekewane ran under the trees to collect the fallen mangoes. They did not take long as Emarr and Bagonoun lay their fish on the ground and helped them fill the baskets. Soon they were off again.

As the sun was setting over the horizon they could hear the crashing of the waves against the rocks. There was a full moon that night, so they had no difficulties finding their way along the shoreline. The cool breeze blowing from the sea was refreshing after the hot humid undergrowth. The tide was out so they walked at a quick pace, later that night they could see the campfires ahead.

The tribe was looking for them and a great cry of joy went out when they were spotted. The tribe ran towards them, happy to see them return safely, and were excited at seeing the milkfish and mangoes.

That night there would be a celebration. They helped distribute the fish and fruit amongst the tribe. Ekewane and Eiru were tired and felt dirty after their long walk. Their hair was tangled and where the branches and pinnacles scratched their bodies, was burning. Ekewane looked down at her grass skirt; it was torn and limp, many of the leaves were torn or missing. The excitement of the day had vanished and now she felt depressed.

She sat down near her mother and small brothers. Her mother wrapped her arm around her to comfort her. She looked around and saw Emarr and Bagonoun surrounded by Emet, Iud and some of the other girls of the village, they were laughing and joking as the boys told them of their adventure.

Ekewane felt the anger escalate; she wanted to scream at them not knowing why she felt this angry. " Emarr was hers! He was the big brother that had died before she was born! He was her friend! What is happening to me? Why do I cry now for any little thing? And always feel so angry?" Ekewane lowered her head sadly and let her hair fall around her face, she felt her eyes stinging, but would not allow herself to cry in front of her tribe.

Then the singing and dancing began. Emet and Iudi, together with the small group of girls started dancing. Ekewane looked at Emet, she swayed to the rhythm of their music, and her body that had been rubbed with scented coconut oil was glittering in the moonlight, her beautiful long black hair was swaying like waves on a calm sea.

On her head was a wreath of frangipani and hibiscus, and around her neck she wore a necklace of pretty shells and feathers. Ekewane looked down at herself and for the first time compared herself to Emet, and felt miserable.

The singing finally ended. Emet and Iud sat next to Emarr and Bagonoun. She watched them laugh together, and felt a deep sense of confusion and sadness within her; and again she asked herself what was happening to her? She could no longer stop the tears from flowing down her face as she got up and went to the small rock pool to bathe, and then slowly walked to her hut. She had not eaten that night; she had not been hungry, even though she had not eaten since they had left the lake.

Emarr had never felt prouder, he had been asked to lead the men back to the lake. Erangue trusted him and had talked to him as an equal.

At the lake he fished with the men. And then when they returned to their village the people treated him like a hero. His parents he knew were proud of him, and the girls wanted his attention. That night he felt important, the girls, Emet, Iudi and others danced and kept looking at him; he could not believe it! Back on their island these girls would never have noticed him -he was from the *Sitio* class and they were from the superior classes.

Emarr and Bagonoun did not want the celebrations to end, as they were the centres of attention of the pretty girls! At one point however, Emarr lifted his gaze as if someone had called his name and watched Ekewane walk slowly to her hut, once she reached her hut he returned his attention to the happy group surrounding him.

# Chapter Thirteen.
## Puberty

Puberty hut.

The sun was high when Ekewane awoke.

Her mother was sitting nearby looking at her strangely.

"Ekewane, we will build you a special hut and you must stay in the hut for a while. We will feed and look after you, and you must not leave the hut."

She was about to ask why, but still felt miserable from the night before, so thought it would be nice not see anyone for a while and be looked after. So lay down again. She did not ask where Eiru was, she felt too tired to care and soon fell asleep again.

When she awoke again her mother and other women of the tribe accompanied her to a small hut near her parents' hut. Her small hut faced inland and she could not see the sea, but could hear the waves as they crashed against the reef. The hut was small and not very sturdy, but inside it was decorated with fine mats and scented flowers.

She was only allowed to leave her hut to go to one of the special rock pools to bathe. Her mother and other women of the tribe prepared special food for her, and massaged her body with sweet-scented coconut oil. Fresh flowers were threaded through her hair and her mats were changed often.

At first Ekewane enjoyed the attention and the fact that she did not have to look after her younger siblings, or carry the water from the pond. At first she felt wonderful, but then started to become restless. She missed her friends. Eiru would come often and visit her and they would play string figures, but Emarr and Bagonoun were strictly forbidden to see her and did not ask Eiru about them.

Ekewane's mother came every day and sat besides her, teaching her the different chants for different spells. She often brought with her various plants and showed her how to grind and mix the potions. Often chants accompanied the blending and healing process.

"One day our people will come to you for help. They may need to heal wounds, but often you will need to call the spirit world to help," explained Emanear.

Ekewane was quiet for a while. She wanted to know more about the spirit world, but was too embarrassed to ask.

Emanear knew that her daughter had many questions to ask so waited patiently. Ekewane was in turmoil, she understood that she was going through a difficult time -a time when she was discovering being a woman and a sorceress.

"Are there many different kinds of spirits?" finally asked Ekewane. Her mother nodded, not wanting to interrupt.

"We will be able to help those who are ill or have been cursed?" Her mother nodded again.

"There were those in our old village that had great powers over the dark spirits?" Her mother nodded again.

"How. How do you cast these spells? Can we cast dark spirit spells?" Ekewane asked silently too embarrassed to look at her mother.

"Yes, we can."

"How?"

"Ekewane, our power is great. We can call on the spirit world to heal or to harm. But the evil spirits are difficult to control. If you call them from the spirit world and use their power, part of them will remain with you. You must decide for yourself what spirits you will call, but remember, our power should be used to help others and not ourselves."

Emanear sat there, her mind drifted to the past when she too had asked her mother these same questions. Her mother had answered her as she did to Ekewane. Her daughter would have to decide her own future; all she could do was to pray to their ancestors to help guide her.

The months passed and finally the day came when her mother said: "You are now a woman Ekewane, and soon we will have to look for a husband."

Ekewane's fear rose, but she controlled her voice and whispered: "I do not want to get married. Why am I so different from the other girls?"

Her mother just put her arm around her shoulders and quietly said: "You do not choose to become a woman, the spirit within you takes you through each stage of your life, you cannot choose . . . you are different from others, but I do not know why."

Ekewane was quiet for a moment, and then asked? " Are Eiru, Emet or Iud women?"

"Emet and Iudi had their celebrations before you, when we were back on our island. I am sorry Ekewane, but although our family is powerful, we belong to the *Ramaoide* class; your ceremony will not show the wealth and power of our family. We cannot kill pigs or chickens they are needed for breeding. I am sorry," she said sadly.

"I don't care about celebrations! I want to leave this hut. I am tired of lying here all day," she thought to herself, but did not speak, not wanting to hurt her mother. Then it occurred to her.

"Do boys also go through this isolation and ceremonies?" she asked curious, wondering if Emarr and Bagonoun were also locked up.

"Yes," replied simply her mother.

"Is that why Emarr and Bagonoun have not visited me?"

"No, both boys have had their ceremonies back on the islands. It is taboo for them to visit you whilst you are in this hut." Then she stood up and looked down at her troubled daughter. "Tomorrow is your last day. Tomorrow night we will have a great celebration."

Ekewane sat there amazed. "A woman, that's why my body is changing!" she thought.

She knew that her body had gone through changes during the past months. She was no longer as thin as before. On her old island she could now marry and have children of her own.

That thought terrified her. She remembered on her island when a woman was pregnant she wore a special mat and was only allowed to eat certain food. The husband also had to eat a special diet, and he was not allowed to cut his hair.

When the baby was due a maternity hut was built and a special birth mat was laid on the floor. During labour, boxes and other closed containers within the hut had to be opened. Soon after the baby was born, both the mother and child were given a little seawater to drink as a cleansing agent. As soon as the baby was born a great celebration would take place.

Ekewane also remembered that many of the women died at childbirth. The thought of marriage and childbirth terrified her, but she knew it was the way of her people, it would be expected of her.

"Ugh!' she yelled frustrated, "I don't want to be a woman! What is ahead of me?"

The next day her mother and other women of the village came to her, rubbed her body with coconut oil and perfume made from sweet smelling flowers on the island. They combed her long black hair with coconut oil until it shone. Her skin had become paler since she had not been in the sunlight for three months and she had put on a little weight. Her mother then gave her a new skirt made of finely woven pandanus threads that felt soft on her body. A belt of dainty shells and small feathers was placed around her waist. A wreath of scented frangipani and hibiscus flowers went around her head. Finally, her mother placed an exquisite necklace made of rainbow coloured shells and long black frigate bird feathers.

"It is nicer than Emet's!" Ekewane thought.

"Why am I comparing myself to Emet? Why do I care?"

She quickly dismissed these thoughts and tried to look like she was enjoying the ceremony, but on the back of her mind was the expectation that was now placed on her. She knew that this was an important and proud event for her parents, she would smile, and anyone looking at her would think she was happy.

The sun was setting and the fires were lit. Ekewane was accompanied out of her hut and placed onto a small stretcher. Then four young men of the village, including Emarr and Bagonoun, carried her around the tribe that had gathered there to celebrate, and then they put the stretcher down beside the large fire. Instead of enjoying being the centre of attention, she felt embarrassed, and cringed as people sang in her honour. The villagers offered her gifts. She was told that she could not give them away as was the custom of other gifts given on different occasions.

Ekewane sat there smiling; she wished the celebrations would end. An abundance of food had been cooked for the occasion. She noticed that there were milkfish and mangoes.

"They have returned to the lake without me," she thought sadly.

The singing continued and then Emet, Iud with the other girls started dancing.

"Ugh!" Ekewane thought again, and looked to see where Emarr was.

He was sitting around the fire next to Bagonoun smiling up at the girls.

"This is supposed to be my celebration!" Ekewane thought angrily. Again she was frightened by the intensity of her feelings. "Why should I care?" she thought again to herself.

The singing and celebrations lasted most of the night. Then at last, her mother led her back to the hut that she had previously shared with Eiru. As she silently walked away with her mother, she did not see Emarr quickly glance up at her.

When Ekewane arrived at her hut, her mother handed her a casket made from pandanus leaves: it was woven with the pattern of their tribe. Her mother then hugged her again and left.

She removed her fine jewellery, and placed them into the small casket. She also had her gifts, put them just inside the door in a basket, and then crawled onto her mat and fell asleep exhausted.

Eiru awakened her as she silently entered the hut and lay down beside her. "I have missed my friend," Ekewane thought, "Eiru is always so peaceful and loving, she is never angry -like me, why can't I be more like her?" And with that thought she fell back to sleep.

# Chapter Fourteen.
## The Cliff

The weeks passed and to Ekewane nothing seemed to be very different than before. Eiru was also isolated into a small hut near her parents, just as Ekewane had been a few months before. Only Eiru was so excited and happy with the right of passage to becoming a woman. Ekewane often joined her in her hut, she envied Eiru's lovely nature: everyone seemed happy to be around her.

In the evenings Ekewane would walk to her favourite spot and wait. Soon Emarr and Bagonoun would come as usual and join her. They never talked much, just sat there quietly each in their own thoughts; they all missed Eiru.

Then finally the day came and Ekewane was excited. She woke up early and ran to Eiru's little hut; tonight she would be free again to share their hut and adventures. She wondered if her parents had planned to find a husband for her soon. In their old village her husband would most likely have been picked out long before now.

That night Eiru was beautiful and glowing. "She is much prettier than Emet," Ekewane thought.

Ekewane sat near her friend and could see that

she was happy. The other members of the tribe brought her gifts. They had finally been able to kill a pig and some chickens and everyone was happy. The island had been good to them. They had plenty of food.

"It is not right that we could not kill chickens or a pig for your celebration, but we can for Eiru. You are of a higher rank than she," said Emanear wistfully.

Ekewane just smiled at her mother, she did not mind, she was happy for Eiru. Eiru was her best friend; she was the only girlfriend she really ever had. Back on her island she would play and swim with her friends the other Emarr and Amweb. They would swim amongst the reef and catch fish. She did not want to join the girls of her tribe, comb their hair and play string figures, but preferred to run free with the boys. But here Eiru preferred her company to the other girls of the village. Ekewane felt happy that she was her friend.

At the celebrations Ekewane looked around without thinking to see where Emarr and Bagonoun were. Emet, Iudi and other girls, as usual surrounded them and they were laughing together and she wondered why the boys never joined her and Eiru when there was a celebration. But Eiru was so happy and she felt her friend's happiness;

all angry thoughts had disappeared that night. However, every now and again she would glance over at Emarr and Bagonoun, and noticed that Bagonoun would often glance shyly across at Eiru.

The days quickly passed. Their days were filled with fishing for octopus along the reef, collecting shellfish and water. At night the four friends would meet at their spot and talk until it was time to return to their huts.

They could still hear the loud piercing screams from the mountain. The tribe would always stopped what they were doing. The spirit, although frightening, had not come any closer to harm them. Some nights Ekewane thought she could hear other spirits outside her hut in the bushes, or wandering through the tall pinnacles near-by, then she would huddle closer to Eiru, who always seemed to sleep peacefully and not hear anything.

There were changes within the tribe. They had started out as disgruntles and angry whispers. The men seemed to be always arguing and Ekewane knew that at the centre were her father and Ramanmada. The tribe was now coming apart; some of the adults seemed to be on her father's side, whilst others agreed with Ramanmada: she could not understand why.

"I will go back up into the mountain!" Ekewane stated frustrated, "I am tired of listening to the adults argue." The four had been sitting quietly at their spot as they did every evening.

"Yes," agreed Emarr and Bagonoun.

Eiru did not say anything and sat there quietly. Ekewane had expected the others to object, after the last frightening episode on the mountain, was surprised at their agreement.

Bagonoun had never been on the mountain, and although the spirits that lived there frightened him, was excited to explore more of the island. He had not been with the three when they went last time and felt he had missed out on their adventure.

"We will not go as far this time. There are some cliffs up the southern side of the mountain. We have seen them when we were fishing in the canoe. Do you remember Bagonoun?" Bagonoun nodded in agreement.

He was hoping to go away a few nights but the cliffs would be better than staying here waiting and not knowing what they were waiting for.

"We will go south along the shore-line until we can find a way up the mountain." Emarr continued.

Early next morning, before the sun rose, the four friends met on the reef. They walked silently along the reef, each in their own thoughts glad to be going away from the tensions that were building up in their tribe. They continued following the coast until the sun was high up in the sky.

"We will sit there beside the undergrowth and eat," said Emarr looking around.

They sat down and he pulled out of the pouch that he always wore pieces of fish wrapped in leaves and handed a piece to each. They had only sat down for a few minutes when he got up and walked towards the undergrowth. The others, as they knew that they were meant to follow, quickly followed.

The climb was steep and difficult. The forest was lush with tropical vines and bushes, and the girls struggled to keep up with the boys who kept walking without looking back. Ekewane did not want to complain; it had been her idea, so she looked at Eiru and smiled. She noticed that Eiru was also hot and tired; there was no sea breeze here under the canopy. Ekewane extended her hand and helped Eiru up the ascent.

For how long they kept climbing she was not sure.

She could not see the boys anymore, but their voices told her that they were not that far ahead. The track they left to follow was easy, and the girls kept walking, even though their legs were burning.

"The sun is high in the sky," Ekewane thought.

Every now and again she could see rays of sunlight streaking through the eerie forest. She felt very thirsty and wondered how long before they could drink.

At a certain point she stopped and said: "I can't hear the boys anymore. Do you think that we are so far behind?"

Eiru did not answer, she thought if she stopped it would be very hard for her to get up again. So they kept climbing.

A little further up the track stopped climbing and crossed the side of the mountain. It was a little easier, and so they could walk faster.

Finally, they stepped out of the undergrowth to a small clearing. Emarr and Bagonoun were sitting there smiling up at them. The girls stumbled over and dropped to the ground exhausted. Emarr and Bagonoun held up two coconuts ready to drink. The girls took the drinks and greedily swallowed the sweet liquid. When they had drank their coconut dry, the boys laughed and handed them another. This time the girls savoured the wonderful juice as they sipped it slowly.

"Emarr and Bagonoun had time to climb the nearby coconut trees and cut some down, we must have been very slow," thought Ekewane.

The four sat there for a time and rested. They felt happy as they looked out over the sea. The cliff was high above the reef, and they could see the steep climb they had had to travel, but felt at peace away from the tension of the tribe. They lay down tired; the heat of day lulled them into a restful slumber. The tribe often slept in the afternoons, it was too hot to fish or do anything strenuous.

Ekewane was the first to awake. She stretched, stood up and looked over the vast sea to where there was a faint line where the sky met the sea. She gazed lazily at the shimmering water; out on the horizon it was hazy. Suddenly she felt her body go cold. Out there far away she saw a monstrous bird, she could see the white of the wings and the large black body shaped like a canoe. How could a canoe be so big with large white wings?

"Look!" she cried pointing at the image in the distance.

The other three woke up startled, and jumped up. They followed the direction of her extended hand, but could see only sea and sky.

"It's gone," she said, her voice still shaky.

"What had she seen? Was it the spirit of her ancestors coming to the island?"

"It must have been one of the very big white birds that fly across the sea," stated Emarr more confidently than he felt. He then put his arm around her shoulders, for he could see that she was still trembling.

Ekewane felt comforted by his arm, but inside her she felt afraid. "Was this a warning?" she thought.

.

# Chapter Fifteen.
## The Frigate Bird Game

*The frigate bird and roost*

It was easier to go down the mountainside. The girls kept slipping trying to keep up with Emarr and Bagonoun, they would laugh and keep going. Ekewane's sight of the mysterious bird was forgotten.

They reached the camp before sunset. Emarr was right it was not that far away, and nobody had noticed their disappearance. However, they felt something had happened whilst they were away, so Ekewane went to find her mother.

"The men have formed teams and are going to go to the other side of the island and catch the frigate birds. And women are not allowed to go!" She looked meaningfully at her daughter. Ekewane was about to complain but thought better of it.

That night as the four met at their usual place she asked Emarr, "Will you and Bagonoun go to catch the frigate birds?"

"Yes" both boys answered proudly. "First we will have to prepare and build two bird roosts, and we will have to sleep in a special place."

"Why can't we come?"

"Because women are taboo! We will not be able to eat fish, only eat coconuts." replied Emarr.

It was called a game, but he knew that it could become very serious. The tension within the tribe had escalated and the 'game' could become dangerous. He was glad Ekewane and Eiru were not allowed to be there; it could get out of hand. He had seen men kill themselves after loosing the game. It was not so much the ability of each player, but went deeper; those that won were believed to have the strongest more powerful ancestors, and the losers were made to feel inferior. Emarr and Bagonoun had never played the game before; only selected men of the tribe could play. However, they had been allowed to watch.

The next morning her mother was sitting alone in her hut and Ekewane joined her. Their ancestors' bones were still in the casket, they had not buried them in front of the hut, because were not sure if they would remain there, or build their hut somewhere else around the island. She was sitting rocking backwards and forwards chanting. Ekewane knew that her mother was calling the spirits of her ancestors to come from the spirit world. She felt a slight tremor and a little anxious, but sat down beside her mother and joined in her chant.

For how long they remained there she did not know. She had lost track of time. She felt her spirit leave her body and float high above in the sky, looking down at the huts and people below. She saw Emarr and Bagonoun fishing in their canoe. She saw Eiru gathering dry wood ready for the night fire. She saw children playing in the rock pools, and still she soared high above the island. She saw that the island was not vey big; a lot smaller than her old island. The lake they had found was large and sparkling under the clear blue sky. She flew higher to the top of the mountain. The leaves of the enormous tomano trees swayed with the breeze, and then her spirit circled around the island and slowly came down.

Her eyes opened wide in wonder. She had not been afraid flying free high above in the sky, and wondered if once her spirit left her body that is the way she would feel - death then would not be so terrifying. Ekewane looked at her mother surprised.

"Your spirit left your body," she smiled and then stood up and left the hut.

"Her mother knew! Had she also soared above in the sky like a bird?"

That night as the four sat at their place, they were all subdued, each thinking about the frigate bird catch. Ekewane and Eiru looked worried and Eiru asked, "How do you catch the frigate bird?"

Bagonoun explained: "There are two teams.

Two men from each team throw pieces of fresh fish in the direction of the wild frigate bird flock: They have to entice the birds to fly down low. These two players are not allowed to catch the frigate birds. The men that will play the game will have one knee to the ground and when the bird is near, he will throw his sling."

"Like the one I used to catch the noddy birds, do you remember?" continued Emarr.

Both the girls nodded.

" The man will aim at the bird's feet and try to snag and entangle its legs. Then pull the string so the bird will fall down. Then they run to it and tie its wings. But it depends on where the bird will fall; it must fall on the area assigned to each team. The frigate birds will then be tamed and kept on a roost in front of the chief's hut," continued Emarr.

None of the four spoke, each was visualizing the game.

"Why can't I come?" complained again Ekewane.

"Because you are a woman!" replied Emarr exasperated.

That night in her hut she did not think about the frigate bird game, but the sensation she felt when she was flying in the air that afternoon. Eiru was asleep she could hear her peaceful breathing. "She is probably dreaming of Bagonoun," and smiled to herself.

Ekewane thought about her mother and grandmother. She knew they were sorceresses; the women of her family had always been sorceresses. She knew that there were two types of sorcerers, some would use plants and massage for healing the body, but the others more powerful could contact the spirits. Her mother was one of the few that could do both, and she felt proud that these skills and power were flowing within, and as if to agree with her the high-pitched shriek screamed louder than ever in the night sky.

That night it rained. Ekewane woke up to the sound of the rain on the roof of her hut. She loved the rain, it was reassuring; the trees would flower and there would be fish. She remembered her island and why they had left, it had not rained for many years.

The morning brought with it a clear blue sky and a hot sun. The men were packing long thin branches and other belongings. Ekewane stood a little distance away watching them and felt sad: "Why am I a woman?" she murmured to herself. She still hated thinking herself as one, but others now saw her that way, so she just sighed turned around, and headed for their place. She sat there silently, already missing her friends.

"Emarr!"

He just smiled at her and sat beside her. They did not speak, but Ekewane was happy just for him to remember her before he left.

"Be good Ekewane, don't go up into the mountain without me," he touched her arm, smiled and left. She felt again a deep stirring within her; Eiru made her feel peaceful, Bagonoun made her laugh and Emarr could always make her feel safe and cared for. She loved her friends, "I will never let them go," she thought stubbornly to herself.

The days went by very slowly. In the evenings she would sit with Eiru in their favorite place. Eiru was often very quiet and Ekewane knew that she too missed their friends, and wondered what they were doing. She wished she could fly again and see the men play the frigate bird game, but somehow knew that she was unable to use these strange powers whenever she wanted to.

All was not peaceful in the camp. Emet and Iud always snickered when they walked past. Ekewane wondered again why they did not like her; true she did not like them, but in her defence had never spoken to them. Emet would often make comments like "Your family think they are better than others but you are not." Or, "you think Emarr prefers you to me, just look at yourself you think and act like a boy! He only sees you as a boy! Then she would laugh. Ekewane did not mind being seen as a boy. She was happy that Emarr liked her as he liked Bagonoun.

One day she saw Emet and Iud whispering to Eiru and felt angry. "They can't say Eiru is a boy! She is sweet and lovely and never says anything hurtful about anyone!" She stomped across to where the girls were speaking, but Emet and Iud had seen her coming and walked away laughing.

"Eiru, are you all right?" Eiru looked at her and just nodded and they walked away together.

That night Ekewane curious asked: "What did Emet and Iud say to you?"

"They just said you were unnatural, neither girl nor boy, they said I should join them and the other girls."

"W-what did y-you say?"

"You are my friend no matter what they call you," she replied smiling.

Ekewane hugged her friend and put her head on her shoulder. "You are my closest friend."

The two girls stayed there for a while longer, then decided they would go to bed. They missed Emarr and Bagonoun.

The day finally came when they saw in the distance the men returning. Ekewane and Eiru joined the other members of the tribe and ran towards them. She saw her father walking in front of the group, he was laughing and joking with the other members of his team. Further behind walked the second team; they were solemn walking with their heads sagged down.

"I told you that our ancestors are the more powerful!" her father's voice boasted loudly, wanting all the tribe to hear. He was the head chief and he knew it. "Emanear! You and the other women prepare a feast in honour of our victory," he laughed. "The other team are weak! Their ancestors are not as powerful as ours!" he continued to call out.

That night there was a great celebration in honour of the winners. The losing team did not show up, but Ramanmada had little choice but to attend. He was the leader of the other team, he had to be there and listen to the insults and taunts thrown at him. Ekewane did not enjoy the celebration, so sneaked away to her favourite spot. She had not spoken to Emarr or Bagonoun since they had returned.

When she reached their spot she was surprised to see both the boys sitting there waiting. Eiru was also there; she had not seen them leave and sat down next to the other three.

"You won," she said flatly.

She was happy for them, but deep inside she felt that things in the tribe were not going to get any better. The image of the blood pouring out of the bodies of the men of her tribe still haunted her.

"We won, but there are troubles ahead. This game was the start of things to come, and I am afraid for our tribe," said Bagonoun.

The other three nodded in silence. Ekewane's heart beat faster and faster, she could see the blood from her tribe, it was drowning her, and it became more difficult to breathe.

But then she felt her hand being squeezed lightly, a much bigger warmer hand was holding hers and she forgot the image and felt safe again.

# Chapter Sixteen.
## Unrest comes to Volcanic Island

*Canoe carved from tomano tree.*

"Foolish men! Why do they have play silly games and then get so very angry?" thought Ekewane as they were walking back to their huts.

The girls entered and lay down on their mats; it was still very hot so they both lay there listening to the sea until it lulled them to sleep.

The days went by and more canoes had arrived from different islands. No longer were her people afraid of the new arrivals. Just as Bagonoun's family had come from another island with similar stories of drought and hardship, so too did these newcomers.

The new arrivals often spoke a different language, but many words could be understood and they quickly became part of the wider tribe. At night her people would gather around and listen to strange stories and legends told by the newcomers. The newcomers also brought with them sago and taro roots. The rains came regularly and the roots that were thought to be dead had germinated and could be harvested. A year had passed since they first arrived on the island.

Ekewane could feel the tension within the tribe. For a while the newcomers seemed to have stopped the tension from rising to the surface, but eventually it returned.

The newcomers also brought with them a new drink made from the coconut tree. They showed the men how to make the drink from unripened coconut buds. The men would climb up to where the coconut buds were still growing, and make a small cut at the bottom of these buds and then tie a coconut shell to collect the sap. Then they waited until it fermented; they called it 'toddy'.

One night there was a celebration, the toddy was ready to drink. After they ate, everyone sat around the large fires and the men handed around some of the toddy in coconut shells. Ekewane was sitting next to her friends curious at this strange drink, the liquid in the shell was handed to Emarr, and she shivered.

"No!" she whispered to Emarr "it is evil, do not drink it!" She did not know why she had said this, and felt embarrassed.

Emarr looked at her in surprise. Ekewane felt mortified, stood up and quickly walked away. Emarr watched her walk towards her hut and sighed. Sometimes he did not understand her, why was this drink evil? He looked around at the other men drinking and laughing, and then looked down at the grey liquid unable to decide. He sighed and then handed the cup to the man sitting beside him. Nobody had noticed Ekewane's warning, everyone seemed happy and laughing.

The merriment continued all night. Ekewane could hear the laughter from her hut, she still felt embarrassed at her warning to Emarr and lay listening to the ocean, and the breeze that was blowing the leaves on the roof of her hut and eventually fell asleep.

The sun rose over the horizon Ekewane stepped out from her hut; she looked around the reef but could only see a few women and the children bathing and playing in the rock pools.

"Where are the men?" she thought. She walked towards the sea and bathed in the warm clear water of a rock pool. When she got out of the water she noticed her mother coming towards her.

"Ekewane some of the men will go up the mountain to the tall tomano trees, they will cut out from the branches new canoes so they can catch more fish. Our tribe is now very large and the men have to catch more fish in order to feed all the tribe. Your father will go with them and they will be away for many days." Her mother sighed and left.

Ekewane wondered if Emarr and Bagonoun would also have to leave and went off in search of them. They were not hard to see, as many of the men still slept even though the sun was now high in the sky. When she reached where they were sitting she asked,

"Will you go with the men to the top of the mountain?"

Both the boys nodded and smiled. "We will have our own canoe," said Bagonoun excitedly.

Ekewane looked at both the boys with envy: "Why do they always have the fun!" she thought angrily as she walked away.

She did not hear Emarr run after her. When he reached her he whispered: "Be safe Ekewane . . . and don't do anything foolish while we are away." He then smiled, turned and ran back to Bagonoun.

The days passed and still the men had not returned from the mountain. Ekewane and Eiru sat at their spot every night but did not speak, each with their own dreams.

One evening they walked towards their place and saw Emet and Iudi sitting there laughing. Ekewane hated seeing the other two girls there; this was their place!

"I will marry Emarr and Iudi will marry Bagonoun," Emet said smugly, and then both girls laughed and walked away.

Ekewane and Eiru felt devastated; had the girls' parents' gone to the boys' parents to ask if they wanted to marry their daughters, as was the custom of their tribe?

"Why do we have to get married?" Ekewane asked angrily.

That night it rained and the girls wondered where their friends were. But they did not have to wait long to see them again. As the morning lingered on Ekewane and Eiru were walking along the reef with some of the other women. They had caught some large octopus and towed them behind on a string. Ekewane was busy trying to pull a large octopus that would not come out of its hole.

"The men are back!" yelled one of the women nearby.

Ekewane and Eiru, together with the women and children on the reef ran towards the men still in the distance, the octopus forgotten and left lying on the reef; they would pick them up on the way back.

When they reached the men everyone was excited. The men showed the new canoes, as well as pandanus fruit and noddy birds. That night there would be another celebration. The group walked together happily to their village. Once Ekewane and Eiru greeted their fathers they looked for Emarr and Bagonoun. The boys were proudly smiling at them; they had built their first canoe and felt proud and excited.

That night everyone seemed happy. The men had

returned with many canoes; now more men could go out over the reef to the deep waters. Fishing from the reef was the women's domain, and although the men were not strictly forbidden, they rarely fished from there.

The next few days were peaceful. Ekewane and Eiru sat together with some of the older women and wove their mats and baskets, at night they watched the men in their canoes fishing off the reef. The men would light their flaming torches and catch the flying fish with nets tied to long poles; the same nets used to catch noddy birds.

"I wish I could be out there on the canoe with Emarr and Bagonoun!" stated firmly Ekewane.

Eiru shuddered at the thought; the sea beyond the reef was very deep and dangerous, and it was taboo for women to fish from the canoe and beyond the reef.

The temporary peace within the tribe did not last for long. The unrest within the larger tribe was again building up. The men had to go further around the island in order to catch more fish to feed the tribe. The coconuts around the site were also becoming scarce and so groups would also go further around the island or up the mountain to gather them.

One night the villagers were informed that there

would be an urgent tribal meeting with all the families. The fire was built and the older members of the tribe sat around it, Emarr's father was also amongst the men. The younger members were allowed to attend, but had to sit around in an outer ring.

Ekewane and Eiru felt apprehensive, they did not know what this meeting was going to be about, so they sat there with the rest of the tribe and waited for the men to speak. Emarr and Bagonoun sat next to the girls silently; they also were wondering the reason behind this urgent meeting.

It was Erangue that spoke first. "We are now many in this tribe. We know that the spirits of the island will not harm us, and the people who arrive are like us and have become part of our tribe. We are safe in our new home."

Nobody spoke; even the smaller children listened even if they did not understand what he was saying, but the tone of his voice commanded their attention.

"The time has come. Our tribe has become too big to live together. We the elders have spoken. We will live in different hamlets according to our families. Each family will become a tribe and those that arrived from other islands may choose to which tribe they want to belong.

Each hamlet will have a tribal name and totem."

Everyone was silent. Ekewane looked around and realised what her father had said was correct. She had not noticed, but the tribe now were many, too many to count, for they stretched far in the circle around the elders. There were only a few when they had first arrived, now there were about a hundred!

The men spoke and argued all night. They were deciding where their families would live, where those members that had not come from their island would belong? At one point Ekewane and Eiru yawned, they were tired and so stood up and went to their hut. Many of the other women and children also left. The elders would let them know when they had made decisions.

The next morning Eiru woke Ekewane up. She was excited and wanted to know where they would live. Ekewane was afraid that they would not be together; her friends may have to move far away and so dreaded the outcome of the meeting. Eiru was impatient and when she realized that Ekewane was in no hurry, ran out to find someone that could tell her the news.

Ekewane got up slowly, went down by the sea and bathed, as was her habit. She then looked around. "The men must be still asleep, they must have talked all night," she thought. "There are only women and children up." She was not sure where she should go so she walked without thinking to her favourite place and waited.

Her friends must have known that she was there so they too went to join her. Ekewane smiled as she saw them coming - but her heart was racing very fast, she was afraid of the news they would tell her.

"You will remain here at this bay with all of your family," smiled Emarr. His brown eyes sparkling, as he watched Ekewane's worried expression.

She turned to Eiru. "And you?"

Eiru smiled, "I am part of your family," she said proudly.

"Your father was the first to land here, so he has the right to choose to remain," said Bagonoun.

Ekewane was happy that Eiru would remain with her, but waited anxiously to hear where Emarr and Bagonoun would live.

"We will both live in the next hamlet!" Emarr laughed unable to keep Ekewane in suspense any longer. "We will be close so we can still all meet here at night."

"Why are you becoming part of Emarr's family?" asked Eiru talking to Bagonoun.

"Because my father and Emarr's father have become good friends, they are always fishing together, just like Emarr and me," he smiled broadly showing his joy at the news.

"But we found the lake as well," said Ekewane. "Who will live there?"

"Ramanmada's family; Emet and Iud." Both boys smiled at Ekewane's expression.

Ekewane at first felt angry. "Why should they have the lake, we discovered it?" She was irritated that Emet would live near the beautiful still water.

"You cannot live everywhere! Would you rather the lake or the sea? Anyway now you will not have to see Emet and Iud every day!" Emarr laughed and the four friends felt happy with each other's presence. They would not live in the same hamlet, but they would still be very close.

Emarr also had another greater joy. He felt that his life was now complete; his family owned land and they were no longer considered from the *Sitio* class.

Ekewane bowed her head and silently thanked her ancestors who had answered her prayers.

# Chapter Seventeen.
# The Abduction

*Sacred rock pool.*

Over the next few weeks the tribes went their
separate ways. Nobody was in a hurry to leave and a
sense of sadness and loss covered the village. Although
they would be on the same island, everybody knew that
things were changing. They felt anxious; they would

have been safer together because of their large number - now they would be more vulnerable.

At last Ekewane's tribe was left on their own. She looked around and saw that there were only 20 people remaining. She had never thought about who was her family, because she had always felt that the tribe was one big family. But at least Eiru did not leave, and Emarr and Bagonoun were close by.

Ekewane remembered the day when Ramanmada's tribe left; she was watching Emet and Iud feeling that at least there was one good thing about the tribes leaving. When Emet ran back to her and said in a smug voice:

"He will marry me, my parents have already decided; Emarr will be my husband. No man wants to marry you!" She laughed as she ran back to join the rest of her tribe.

Ekewane felt as if Emet had hit her. "What do I care what they think!" she thought angrily to herself. She turned away and hastily walked to the place she knew she would find peace.

A few weeks later as Ekewane was sitting with the other women of her tribe weaving their tribal mats and baskets, she was watching a white tern flying in circles over their small settlement.

"We are going to have a birth within our tribe," said her mother and smiled at the other women, who laughed aloud.

Ekewane shivered, but wondered how her mother knew this.

"The white tern has been sent by the spirit world with joyous news. They are messages of happiness and birth," explained Emanear. "It will be a time of great celebration for all of the island. The first born on this island will be known to all those that are to be born in time to come."

One evening some days later as the four friends met at their usual place, the boys were describing their day.

"We were diving off the reef, fishing the large eels, and looking at the holes in the reef where the eels hide and we came across a large underwater open cave: it was dark and gloomy. The cave was very big and we could swim in it. As it was dark, we decided to leave that place and fish further along the reef," explained Bagonoun thoughtfully. He did not know why, but the cave frightened him.

"You have seen part of the spirit world. There are tunnels under the island that lead to different holes. You must stay away from these holes. If you enter the spirit world you will not be allowed to return," whispered Ekewane. In her mind she could see these dark tunnels, one of the holes that lead from the tunnel was at the lake, she had seen it and felt the force within.

The other friends listened and shuddered: they did not doubt her. And from a distance they heard those shrieking piercing screams – as if to confirm her words. The four friends did not speak any more about the caves. They sat there watching the gentle waves over the reef, and the flames from the torches of the fishermen catching flying fish with their nets beyond the reef.

The next morning fierce angry shouting woke Ekewane and Eiru up. Their hearts were beating loudly - were they being attacked? Their tribe was now small and the other tribes may not reach them in time? The girls thought as they ran out of their hut.

Ekewane also remembered the large bones found by the lake. "Maybe these large monsters had been hiding and now saw that their tribe was weak had come to kill them?"

They have taken it! Ramanmada has always been jealous of my armband! He has always been jealous of my power!"

Ekewane had never seen her father so angry. All the clan surrounded their angry chief.

"We will attack him and kill him for stealing my shell armband!"

She stood there petrified. The image of the blood from the people lying on the ground was still vivid.

"NO!" she screamed.

The tribe turned around and looked at her curiously. Her father was stunned, and for a moment forgot his angry outburst. His daughter had dared raise her voice over his, the chief! He looked at her unable to find the words to say to her.

Ekewane's mother also looked at her and then her husband and understood that she had to intervene. Her daughter had put herself in a dangerous position; she had humiliated her father.

"Ekewane has great powers! She has the gift given to her by my grandmother. She has seen the blood lost between our people."

Everyone was silent and even though Emanear spoke quietly, the people were in awe as they looked at Ekewane.

"Had her mother also seen the blood?"

Ekewane felt uncomfortable all her eyes were looking at her, waiting to see what else she would say. She felt the blood rush to her face as she lowered it, and let her long hair hide as much of it as she could.

It was Emanear's voice that spoke again as she turned to her husband.

"We do not know who has taken the armband. We have not seen any strangers amidst our family. If any of Ramanmada's tribe were nearby, we would have seen them. It may have been the spirits that took it. In this our new home . . . you have no need to show your power. There are no traders from other islands that visit us," she said sadly. "The shell armband belonged to another place. It is not needed here and at this time of our people. It will return again when it is needed."

Erangue was silent for a very long time.

"So it shall be," he announced.

He had never questioned the powers of his wife, but now another feeling flooded through him. He was angry with Ekewane for interrupting him whilst he was speaking, but he was proud that she would one day be a powerful sorceress for his tribe – even more powerful than Emanear? He thought proudly. In the future our tribe will need all of the powers from the spirit world.

Ekewane will own this land as is the custom of our tribe, and we need to find her a strong husband to help her lead this tribe when our ancestors come to take me.

A few days had passed when her parents asked her to join them. They were sitting in front of their hut waiting. Ekewane felt nervous, she did not know what they had planned to talk to her about, but she felt uncomfortable.

"Ekewane, there comes a time in our lives when we must find a partner, it is the way of our people," said her mother softly.

Ekewane felt the anger rise up inside her. She did not want to hear anything about marriage, but she knew not to speak.

"Your tribe is very powerful. There are many men on this island, so the girls have many strong men to choose from," continued her mother.

Ekewane felt her face burn. "So much for Emet's

prediction!" she thought to herself.

"We will find you a suitable husband," continued her father.

"No!" she whispered "I do not wish to marry!" the tears were now running down her face. "Could her parents not understand, she did not want to marry, it was too soon!"

"It is too early for a husband," murmured Ekewane too afraid to look at her parents. "Please!" she lifted her head and looked pleadingly at her parents.

Erangue looked at his wife, he felt confused and uncomfortable. Ekewane was his oldest child and he loved her and did not want to see her this distressed.

"Ekewane, it is the way of life, we must marry and continue our tribe." Emanear looked again at her daughter. She did not understand her; other girls were excited when their parents told them they would find them a husband.

"This island will bring many changes to our tribes and our traditions. Ekewane has seen the future and she does not want to marry. What has she seen? What will the future bring to our people?" Emanear thought sadly. She looked at her husband and then turned to Ekewane.

"We will speak again Ekewane, but you must marry."

Erangue looked confused at his wife but did not say a word. He watched his daughter stand up and sadly walk away.

"Why does she not want a husband?" he asked his wife confused.

Emanear answered quietly, "The times of the past are changing."

Emanear and Erangue sat there silently watching their daughter walk away towards the sea.

Ekewane did not say anything to her friends that night. She sat there listening to the boys laughing and talking about their day, and she thought angrily. "They can go out on their canoes and fish the large fish; we can only fish from the reef. They can dive deep under the sea beyond the reef –it is forbidden for us to go there! Why is this so?"

Emarr must have known that she felt disturbed, and although he did not ask her what was wrong, he just wove his fingers through hers. Ekewane felt the warmth of Emarr's hand, she felt Eiru quietly sitting next to her and Bagonoun happily describe their day, and cast a heavy sigh.

"I do not want things to change, I want to stay with my friends," she thought sadly.

That night as she lay in her hut listening to the wind howling as if warning her, she felt apprehensive. She shivered and felt her body cold with fear. "This is silly!" she thought, but huddled closer to Eiru who was fast asleep.

She must have fallen asleep because she was brutally awoken. She could not breathe, strong rough hands were over her mouth and her arms and legs were held firmly so she could not move. It was dark and she could only make out the shadows of two men.

Ekewane thought that someone had come to kill her, her last thought was for Eiru. "Please don't kill her!" she screamed in her mind, then felt herself fall deeper and deeper into a black void; she could not fight so she let the darkness overwhelm her.

She felt as if she was swimming in a sea. At times she could feel and hear the world around her, and at times she returned to the blackness.

When she was conscious, she felt a sharp pain around her wrists and feet; something was cutting into them. Her body was being carried. Her lungs struggled to breathe; she felt an acute pain in her chest when she tried.

All night long her body swayed with the movement of her captors as they walked silently up a steep track, at times almost dropping her, as they lost their footing. On and on they walked.

At times when she was awake, she would try to escape the pain and concentrate on happier memories. But could not, fear overwhelmed her. She tried not to remember the strange frightening stories, of how girls were sacrificed to the spirit world, and felt even more terrified, and then she would drift off again in the black world of her mind, where there were no feelings of pain or fear.

When she finally awoke from her dreamlike state, she found herself tied to a pole in the middle of a small hut. She looked around and saw that the tiny hut had no openings and wondered where she was.

She tried to stop her heart from beating so loudly, so could hear the noises outside. She listened carefully between the deafening beat her heart was making, and could hear the murmur of water, and the hushed voices of people speaking quietly.

Ekewane struggled to break loose, but the ropes cut even deeper into her arms and legs.

The sun was up, the faint rays were filtering through the leaves of her hut, then there was an opening to her side and a shadow crawled in.

Ekewane looked horrified at the shadow which entered her hut. At first could not recognise them, but as her eyes adjusted to the light she recognised the person leaning over her holding a drink to her mouth.

She was so stunned that she did not scream and let the cool water flow down her scorched throat.

"Don't be afraid Ekewane, nobody will harm you," quietly whispered Eyouwit, Emet's mother.

Ekewane tried to ask "Why?" but when she opened her mouth no sound came out.

Eyouwit did not say anything else to her and then turned around and left her alone again.

Ekewane tried to think why Ramanmada was holding her hostage, surely if they wanted to attack her father's tribe they would have, why was she been held captive?

She lay there waiting, trying to ignore the

throbbing pain, hoping that someone would come and explain why she was there. For how long she waited she could not tell.

The hut was gloomy, only a few rays of surreal light streaking through, which cast ghostly shadows around her.

Then finally she heard a rustle from where Eyouwit had entered. The thatched door was lifted and two men crawled in. For a moment she wondered how two large men could fit into this small hut?

"You will marry my son Ioopu," said Ramanmada.

Ekewane looked horrified, she was captured so she would marry! She felt like laughing did they not know she would not marry anyone! Especially Emet's brother!

"I- will -marry -no - one," she said in a hoarse voice. "My father will find you and he will kill you!" she tried to sound forceful, but her throat hurt and the only sound that came out was a frightened whisper.

"Your tribe will think you have run away! They will not look for you. You have run away before and they will not look for you for many days. You are reckless and unpredictable, but marriage will change you!" Ramanmada laughed at her.

"By the time your tribe will find you, you will be married to Ioopu, and they will accept your marriage." With this final sentence he crawled out of the hut.

Ioopu looked at Ekewane, he wished it could have been done another way, but his parents had approached her parents and they had refused. She was the great chief's daughter and one day she would own most of Erangue's tribal land, as well as being a powerful sorceress and she had to be his wife.

Ekewane was angry, she was so angry she wanted to scream and scream, but her throat hurt and she could barely move her hurt broken body. Her legs felt numb except for the burning sensation the rope cutting into her ankles made. She had struggled hard to loosen the ropes; she could make out thick black drops of blood coming from the tight ropes.

"I will not eat and die, that is better than marrying Ioopu! And Emet will be my sister? And then she will marry Emarr! And Bagonoun will probably marry Iud! Uggh!" she spoke hoarsely to herself.

During the day Eyouwit brought her milkfish and mangoes and placed then in front of her mouth, but Ekewane just turned her head stubbornly and refused to eat.

The next day she also refused to eat. Ekewane felt wet with perspiration, the heat within the hut was stifling, a cool breeze could not enter the small slits between the leaves. She had not bathed in two days and felt even more desolate.

Ekewane kept drifting in an out of her uneasy muddled dreams. She dreamt that she was in one of the rock pools and felt the warm water flowing over her body as she went into the water, but instead of remaining above the surface of the water, she kept going deeper and deeper. She wondered how she got there and why did she not have to breathe?

She looked around at the numerous coloured fish swimming near her; they were not startled and she smiled at them. She joined in their games swimming in and out of the corals and felt free and happy: "This is where I belong, here there is peace, I feel at peace," she thought and felt the warm water caress her. She played with the fish, first joining one group and then another.

She kept swimming happily, but then she saw a dark hole in one of the corals. At first she thought that she would ignore it like the other small fish around her.

But she was attracted to it, so she slowly, cautiously, swam near the entrance. It was so dark in there, she felt afraid, but an unknown force kept pulling her in. Something dangerous lived in the shadows, but she kept swimming towards it ignoring the warnings.

A dark shape started coming towards her, it had tentacles like the octopus she fished on the reef. She screamed for help, but no sound came from her mouth. She tried to swim away, but knew she was helpless; the current was drawing her closer and closer to the ominous enemy. She was getting weaker and weaker, until she had no more strength to fight the force, so closed her eyes and let the cold current take her. She felt the black tentacle over her mouth and . . . it was warm and familiar!

Ekewane open her eyes startled, she recognised these hands, Emarr! She wanted to scream out his name.

"Hush Ekewane," he whispered.

She nodded and he took his hand from her mouth and felt his shell knife cut through the ropes that were binding her hands, once he had freed her hand he cut through the ones cutting into her ankles.

Emarr gently caressed the side of her face until he reached her lips, and slowly lifted a sweet drink; it was coconut water and she swallowed it greedily.

She could almost feel Emarr's face turn into a smile as she splashed the water over her face as she tried to swallow it too quickly.

"Ssh, don't be afraid," he whispered. He held her close for a moment, and then pulled her towards the small opening he had cut at the back of the hut. When she felt the cool night air, he lifted her without any effort and walked silently away from the camp. When they had reached the undergrowth she heard another familiar voice.

"Is she all right?" asked Bagonoun concerned.

"Yes," whispered back Emarr, "We must hurry and get far away from the encampment, for they will look for her in the morning."

There was only a small moon that night. The shadows of the trees were frightening, they had walked for several hours and she could feel Emarr getting tired.

"Please let me walk," she whispered faintly.

"You are still weak, I can carry you."

"No, please let me down,' she pleaded.

So Emarr gently placed her on the ground. At first her legs could not hold her up and she fell to the ground. Emarr caught her.

"I told you that you are still too weak," he said impatiently.

"No, let me try again."

"We are a long way from their encampment," said Bagonoun. "Let her try and walk, we can go slower now." She tried to stand again. It took all her strength. The cuts around her ankles burnt, but she was determined to walk on her own.

Ekewane walked very slowly, but the boys were no longer in a hurry. Every now again they would let her sit and rest.

Ekewane noticed that they kept walking higher into the mountainside and wondered where they were going. "It would have been easier to follow the track down from the lake to the sea and then the shoreline," she thought.

"We have taken the long way back, because they will not think you will go this way. It is longer and more difficult, but less dangerous," said Emarr knowing that Ekewane would ask herself why they had taken such a long way back to her village.

All night they walked, often tripping over pinnacles and fallen branches. Emarr was first cutting and shifting branches so that Ekewane would find it less difficult; he was concerned for her, but she was stubborn and so let her walk.

Ekewane struggled behind Emarr although he was walking very slowly. Bagonoun walked behind her, listening for any sound that would tell them they were being followed, even though they doubted Ramanmada would follow them here.

Ekewane felt dizzy, her body ached but still she kept dragging her legs one in front of the other, just as she had done when they had first arrived, and she had helped pull in the canoe from the sea.

In her head she kept chanting the notes her mother had taught her, they helped her withdraw from some of the pain she felt. The sun was now coming up over the horizon, she could see the light of the undergrowth change from a dark green to a sickly yellow green, and then . . . her legs could not hold her any longer and she fell. She felt the cool earth on her face and wanted to remain there, maybe it would be easier if she just let herself go and not open her eyes again. She felt the familiar black world overwhelm her; she sighed and let go.

Emarr looked down at the sleeping girl. Every now and again he would see her trembling.

"I have found her, she is now safe. Ramanmada will not find her here, and will not dare to go near Erangue's village again."

His mind drifted back to the night she had gone missing. He had been asleep when was awoken by what he thought was Ekewane crying. He remembered opening his eyes and seeing her on the other side of the hut; her head between her knees sobbing. Her image a silver misty light, but he knew it was her.

He had jumped up startled, but when he rubbed his eyes to see more clearly all he could see were the silver rays of light from the moon outside. He should have felt foolish, but could not shake the feeling of pain -Ekewane's pain. He had lay down again and listened to the sad murmur of the mountain spirits; they were not screaming tonight, it was a lament.

The next morning he had awoken feeling still

tired- the image of the night still fazed him. Bagonoun wanted to go out in their canoe, but he had persuaded him to dive for fish off the reef instead.

The morning had only begun, he had dived only a few times, and when coming up for air he looked across the reef and saw a young girl hurrying towards them.

He remembered feeling a sense of panic. Eiru looked distressed and he hurriedly walked towards her. Her face told him the story before she explained; something bad had happened to Ekewane.

"She has gone!" whispered Eiru.
Emarr's heart sank, "G-gone?"

"Yes, this morning when I awoke she was gone. I looked everywhere, but I am unable to find her."

Emarr sighed, "She is not dead. The spirits have not taken," he thought.

They did not hear Bagonoun join them. "Maybe she has gone up to the mountain by herself?"

"No! She would not go up there again without us," replied Eiru anxiously.

The three walked towards Eiru's village. When they reached their spot they sat down silently.

"Maybe the spirit world has taken her?" asked Eiru

frightened.

"No, the spirits will take the person's spirit not their body. The body is too heavy," replied Bagonoun confidently.

"But who would want to hurt her? Whoever took her knew which hut she slept . . . there must have been more than one man . . . otherwise, she would have woken you up," Emarr looked at his two other friends. "But who?"

"The only tribe that is hostile to Erangue is Ramanmada," said Bagonoun thinking out aloud.

"We will go to Ramanmada's village!" said Emarr angrily.

"But we are not sure it was him." Bagonoun looked frightened.

"We will go across the mountain and hide near the village and see if we can see Ekewane."

Eiru listened to the two boys make plans. She had wanted to go with them, but they had convinced her that it could become dangerous and they would travel faster without her. And so they had left Eiru sitting there sadly watching them disappear through the undergrowth.

They had travelled all day and when the sun went

down the first night, they lay down and slept. The next morning they hurried again cutting their way through the dense forest. The sun was high in the sky when they could smell the smoke from the village. Shortly after they could see the huts, so they lay there quietly hiding in the thick bushes watching the huts that surrounded the still smoking embers of the fire from the night.

They had waited all morning and watched the villagers go about their daily routines. There seemed nothing suspicious about the village, except for a small hut that had no openings. For a moment Emarr thought that it must have been an initiation hut for the girls of the village, but it must be stifling hot in there!

They kept watching closely in case someone would come towards their hiding place. Emarr's eyes kept returning to the strange hut. At one stage he saw Ramanmada's wife enter with food and then come out soon after.

"It must be the initiation hut for girls," he thought.

But later on that day Ramanmada and his son loopu entered the same hut. His body was sore from lying down all day in the same spot, but when he saw the two men enter the hut, he was filled with anger. He knew that Ekewane was in there, and he wanted to jump out and kill the two men.

Bagonoun must have come to the same conclusion and sensed Emarr's anger; he had laid his hand on his arm and whispered "Later."

They had crawled away from the site. They had to make plans.

That night Emarr would cut through the back of the cut and rescue Ekewane. They would then go back the way they had come, up the mountain.

So late that night when all the tribe were sleeping, he circled the village keeping close to the bushes. He then crawled towards the back of the hut. His heart was heavy as he cut silently through the side of the hut and made a small opening. He looked inside, and when he saw the dark outline of Ekewane lying there, he felt dizzy.

His head was spinning; Ekewane looked so small and helpless with her feet and hands tied. He had to fight to control his temper and act quietly. When he put his hand over her mouth, she was startled, but then must have recognised him, and nodded.

He had to cut the ropes that were binding her and

could feel where the blood had crusted. The ropes had cut deep into her flesh.

"Why did they tie her so tightly?" he thought angrily.

He knew he was hurting her, causing fresh blood to come from the wounds, but still she did not utter a sound, just tensed every now and again when he had to pull the ropes loose.

Hatred filled him, he had never felt such a strong emotion, but for Ekewane's sake he did not react to his hatred and kept calm.

When he had cut her loose he pulled her gently from the hut and lifted her into his arms. She was awake because she curled her thin arms around his neck and held him close.

When he reached the undergrowth Bagonoun was waiting and outstretched his arms to take her, but Emarr did not want to let go of her, so Bagonoun went first and led the way through the side of the thick forest.

As they travelled Emarr's arms ached, but still he would not give her to Bagonoun. Then a small voice had asked him to walk, at first he refused, but then he knew how stubborn she could be, so he gently put her on the ground. They were far from Ramanmada's camp, so they could go slow. They had walked slowly because of Ekewane, every now and again stopping to rest. But as the light was coming into the sky, she had used up all of her strength and collapsed.

Ekewane could see coloured lights flickering in front of her eyelids and thought that she was once again under water swimming with the different multicoloured fish.

She felt something cold and wet against her lips and she drank.

"Ekewane?" asked Emarr gently.

She opened her eyes and looked at Emarr. He was smiling at her, then she turned towards the flickering light; it was a small fire burning.

"D-don't," she panicked thinking that Ramanmada's tribe would see it.

"Don't be concerned, we are in a cave and they will not look for us here. We are a long way from their camp," said Bagonoun confidently.

Ekewane looked around and noticed that they were in a large cave cut within the pinnacles. She could hear water and looked around confused.

Emarr smiled and said: "We have found an underground well. The water is sweet like our pools back home."

They were sitting at the entrance of the cave that led down to a small pond. The cave then continued into the mountain. Ekewane thought that this was another entry into the spirit world, but did not feel afraid. She felt that the spirits had brought them here. So she lay there listening to the trickle of water, the sound was soothing and the cave was cool and she felt safe, only Eiru was missing she thought.

Ekewane felt like she had slept for a long time, she woke up to the smell of meat cooking in the fire and smiled to herself.

Bagonoun was looking at her and asked: "Why are you smiling?"

She did not answer but remembered the last time she woke up with Emarr cooking noddy birds in the fire.

Ekewane tried to eat the meat, but could not; all she could do was sip water. After a while the boys decided they must leave and return her home; they knew that Ekewane was not well and needed her mother's help.

"Can you walk?" asked Emarr worriedly as she insisted in getting up.

"Yes," Ekewane answered more confidently than she felt.

So they helped her up and slowly continued their walk home. However, they had only walked a little way when she collapsed again. Emarr tried to wake her but Ekewane was lost in her dark world.

The boys took it in turns in carrying her, Her body was limp, and although she was only small, was difficult to carry down the steep mountainside.

They finally heard the crashing of the waves and knew that they were almost there. When they came out of the undergrowth they saw people running towards them.

Ekewane parents were there and Emarr handed her over to her father's arms. Emarr was worried that they had taken too long to get her home, and now it was too late, the spirit world had already taken her.

"Take her to the healing pool," whispered Emanear.

Nobody questioned Emanear as she was the only one that could now save Ekewane.

Erangue carried his daughter to a small rock pool not far from their huts. The pool had pinkish water from the algae that grew on the surrounding pinnacles. He gently placed her in the pool, looked as his wife and walked away sadly.

"I need to speak to Emarr and Bagonoun. I must find out what happened . . . and then . . . the anger rose within him . . . I will kill whoever has done this to my daughter," he thought angrily to himself.

Ekewane again drifted in and out of a strange world. She could hear people's voices but could not speak or open her eyes. She had been able to distinguish the different warmth of the boys that carried her, she knew when Bagonoun or Emarr was carrying her.

She had tried to open her eyes, but every time she felt she was floating towards a far away light; the darkness would pull her back again.

She had also felt her father's arms as he carried her to the water. Her body felt warm and safe wrapped in the warm water. She did not know for how long she lay there, but felt the cold air on her body as she was gently lifted up and wrapped in a mat.

The days that followed were very strange for her. She could not feel her body; it was dead. But she watched from above as her mother and other women put coconut milk to her lips and tried patiently to let the drops trickle down her throat.

She saw her mother apply a green paste onto her wounds, but she did not flinch, the body she was watching was a lifeless object not her own. She watched her mother gently massage her body with coconut oil and heard her soothing chant.

She watched as the women carefully carried her body again, and again to the sacred rock pool with the pink water. And still she floated above them watching and wondering why they were so sad. She did not need this body she was content watching her people.

At times she felt a strong pull back to that listless body, but a much stronger force was pulling her away. She did not want to go back, here, she felt free to watch her people from above.

She listened to the endless chant her mother sang to her as she sat beside her, and wanted to ask her mother to let her go. Time and pain did not exist here where she was.

That light became fainter as she drifted," I don't want to return, I am happy here," she thought to herself, as she soared high above in the sky with only the birds around her. But then she looked down at her friends! They were at their place. Eiru was crying and she wanted to go down and comfort her and tell her she was happy and not to be sad.

Then one night she saw someone crawling into her hut. "They have come back to take my body," she thought to herself, but did not feel afraid; the body did not belong to her anymore. She looked more intently; there was something familiar about the person who now sat beside her body holding her hand. She looked closely and saw tears running down his face.

"Emarr," whispered a small voice from the lifeless body.

# Chapter Eighteen.
## Ioopu

Ioopu felt a sharp pain in his chest and his hand went to the source of this pain. He felt a thick sticky liquid between his fingers and for a moment wondered what it could be. He looked across to see if Gope was still there, but the hut was empty.

Ioopu had always been disliked by all of the villagers. His arrogance and bullying had led others of the village to avoid him. For all of his life he had preferred his own company. He was convinced that the other people living in his village were jealous of him, and wanted to take the wealth and po*sition* that was rightfully his.

Ioopu belonged to the prestigious *Enename* class. His father Ramanmada was a chief. His family possessed great areas of land and numbers of coconut and pandanus trees, which meant that they had great power within the village.

Their village was very large; it was comprised of different hamlets. Members of the same family lived in each hamlet and a chief represented them. A chief could be either a man or a woman. The head chief of the village however, had to be voted in by all of the chiefs. The head chief had the power to make decisions in regards to the whole village, whereas, the others could only make decisions for their hamlets.

When he was younger he often enjoyed insulting and picking a fight with the boys from the lower *Sitio* class.

"They are only our servants!" he would state to anyone listening.

There were times when he was younger, that some of the other boys from the two higher classes would join in his banter, but they had eventually become tired of this game and went on to other more interesting pursuits.

Ioopu understood from an early age, that although his parents were rich and powerful, they were not the most powerful family in the village. The great head chief Ekriaro was the most powerful man in the village, and Erangue his son, was also richer and more powerful than his father.

Erangue had been chosen to represent their people when traders from other islands came. He wore that prestigious shell armband; he was the one that the wandering tribes would deal with, exchanging fine pieces of shell money and jewellery.

Ioopu had always felt jealous of this power and felt it unfair that his father did not possess it. Then one day it would become his, as he was the oldest son.

As if this was not sufficient to give Erangue a higher distinction, he had also married one of the richest women from the village, not only did she have land and many coconut trees, but also prestige and respect; she was known for her magic powers; she was the most powerful sorceress in the village.

As the years passed Ioopu's envy had become hatred. He would however console himself knowing that Erangue's oldest son had died.

In later years Erangue did have two more sons, but they were still very young and they too could die, he reasoned to himself. Ioopu often sat and brooded about the injustice of his fate, "I was born to be the head chief!" he would smirk to himself.

Ioopu avoided all the people in the village, even his own family. His parents were concerned about his behaviour. He would sit alone talking to himself, and did not join in with the other boys in their games. But they thought that he would change when he became older.

When Ioopu had gone through puberty, there was a great celebration, even though it had not rained for many years and the people of the tribe often went hungry.

"I am a chief's son. I belong to the *Enename* class, so there must be a great celebration. I am now a man! It is in these times that we must show our wealth. We are above the others and we must show it!" he had declared to his parents.

It was during this period that he met his only friend Gope. With Gope he found a true friend that understood him.

"Not even my parents understand me." Ioopu would often explain to Gope.

As the years passed, Ioopu with the help of Gope, became even more manipulative and cunning, and was unpredictable and often cruel. He would often fight with the other boys he believed were trying to take from him what was his birthright. His greatest ambition was to one day have power over the village. Gope was the only one who understood his worth, and they would often discuss the day the he would become the head chief.

Ioopu, like all the members of the village was governed by the spirit world. They prayed to the powerful spirits of their ancestors for protection and wellbeing. But all knew that the dark spirits were evil and vindictive. The dark spirits were called upon to avenge a wrong, to curse a rival's crop, cause an illness, and even inflict death.

In the shadows of the village, there lived a dark spirit sorcerer. He was the purveyor of evil spells and illnesses. The villagers openly shunned him; he was the embodiment of the dark forces, and they were afraid of him. However, they would secretly visit him when they needed his powers.

The spirits had spoken to loopu and told him that they would help him become the great head chief. So with the help of Gope they had formed a plan; he would learn to use the dark magic. Then as the head chief he would be able to control both the physical and spirit world, and no one could take away what was his by right.

One morning after deliberation with his friend, he decided to carry out his plan. He crept away from his village and went to the old sorcerer's hut.

"I am loopu, son of Ramanmada. The spirits have sent me so you can teach me how to use your powers."

The old man knew who he was, and also knew about his reputation.

"My magic power cannot be given to all!" he stated, eyeing Ioopu suspiciously.

There was something about this boy that intrigued him. He was good at reading a person, and he could sense ambition and something else, he could not recognize.

The old sorcerer looked at him for a moment and thought. "I need an apprentice. I have no children of my own and when I have joined the spirit world, my powers will be lost forever. This boy will be dangerous if he has my power. I need to call upon the spirits and ask them to help me decide,"

"Come back tomorrow, son of Ramanmada and I will give you my answer. I must ask the spirits." And with that he lowered his head and began chanting.

Ioopu looked around the dark hut filled with small vessels containing bones, stones and different vegetations. The hut had a strange pungent smell and he liked it. He got up and walked out silently.

In the forest nearby, Gope was waiting for him, and they discussed what they would do when he had gained the old man's knowledge and power. Ioopu told Gope of the people he would curse when he was able to use the spells.

The person he hated most was Erangue. He would cast a curse on him and Ioopu relished the thought of Erangue's downfall. Gope smiled and agreed with him.

The next morning they set off again to the sorcerer's hut. Gope would wait for him and then they would discuss the potions and spells.

The old man was expecting him. He had called upon the spirits for a long time and they had decided that Ioopu would make a good apprentice.

"We will start," stated simply the old man.

Ioopu had turned out to be a very keen student. When he was not with the old man he would join Gope and dream about his illustrious future; he would become the most powerful head chief the village had ever had.

"No one will be able to stand against me. I will be richer and more powerful than my father, and I will marry the richest women of the village." He would then smile with his friend already anticipating his future.

One day as he watched some of the children play, he noticed a small girl playing with her two friends. She was very small but spirited as she kept up with the two boys. He knew who she was; she was Erangue and Emanear's only daughter Ekewane.

"One day she will inherit all the land and coconut trees belonging to her mother," he smiled pleased at this thought. He compared himself to the other boys of the village, and felt confident that he was the best choice to one day be her husband.

"She is not very pretty, but then you can have many wives!" said Gope when Ioopu discussed his plan.

He sometimes watched Ekewane and compared her to his sister Emett, she was prettier and like the other girls of the village spent a long time caring for herself, whereas Ekewane seemed to be only interested in swimming and fishing like the boys of the village.

"She will change," he would mutter to himself.

When the islanders had first decided that they must leave their island home, Ioopu disagreed with his father. He had argued at length with him, but his father had chosen to leave with some of the other families.

He had then sought out Gope and complained to him. Gope however, convinced him that in the new land, he would not have to compete with Erangue, and his father would be the head chief.

"When your father becomes old, you will be the great head chief in this new land." explained Gope.

Ioopu was surprised that he had actually enjoyed the preparations to leave their island. He knew that those that were not leaving felt envious, so he relished in the thought that he was one of the chosen ones.

The journey however was terrifying. He had lost hope of reaching land and it had seemed his dreams had ended. Then, they were once again safe! The nightmare was over. His dreams would come true; he was destined to be great. But yet again Erangue was first! He had felt so angry, so full of hatred for this chief who was always ahead of them.

Settling into the new island was not exciting for him. He took his rightful place beside his father. He spent most of his time sitting along the reef talking to Gope, or hidden in the undergrowth practicing his chants and spells. The other members of the tribe did not take any notice of took him; they were too busy setting up camp, finding food, and discovering the island.

He had almost hoped to encounter a hostile tribe so that Erangue would be killed. But the island seemed to offer nothing more hostile than the spirits that constantly screamed! He was not fearful of the spirit world, because now he had the power to control them.

Ioopu had noticed Ekewane when he arrived, and his initial plan seemed to be on track again; he would marry her. Here on this island he did not have any competition.

He also noticed that Ekewane had made friends with three others, and he had often crept to where they were sitting at night to listen to their conversations. In the end however, he became bored and decided that he need not be concerned, after all Emarr was one of the *Sitio* class, and Ekewane's parents would never allow such a marriage. The other boy Bagonoun had come from another island, and therefore was not worthy of any thought.

When Ekewane had her initiation ceremony he had informed his parents that he would marry her. They had approached Erangue and Emanear to ask their permission for their son to marry her, as was their custom. Ioopu was sure they would be grateful, but she had refused!

He had felt so humiliated, so angry with her! Who did she think she could marry better! Even though she was chief's Erangue's daughter, and she had inherited her mother's magic, she would never find a better husband!

It was then that he started making plans with Gope. "One day she will be my wife and her powers and land will be mine. I will have many wives, and then she will become their servant. How dare she refuse me!" he assured Gope.

Ioopu's hatred for Erangue had increased. He wanted revenge, so he set about making his curses. He would make Erangue suffer. Then all those that supported him would also be made to suffer. His only concern was Emanear, would her magic be stronger than his?

The opportunity to further carry out his plan arose when the tribes had eventually parted. His father had the second choice to decide where to live, and had chosen the lake. This choice was pleasing to Ioopu, he would be far away from Erangue's village and so his plan could be carried out much easier.

At first his parents opposed his plan, but then he could be so persuasive; he had reminded his father about the frigate bird game defeat. Knowing that his father still felt humiliated and could not live it down, by Ioopu marrying Ekewane they would also inherit her magic and powerful ancestors.

So the plan had come about. Ekewane would marry him, and once they were married, Erangue and Emanear would have to accept the way they went about the marriage, and probably grateful to him for marrying their wild daughter.

"But she had disappeared! How she escaped he did not know, but felt afraid that she had called upon the spirit world to take her away. How powerful was she to be able to command the spirits this way?"

He became fearful to leave his hut and only Gope was always there with him. Every day his mother would bring him food and water, but he never acknowledged her: he sat alone in the dark hut constantly muttering to himself.

# Chapter Nineteen.
## Tribal War

Tribal armour.

Ramanmada was preparing for retaliation from Erangue. He knew that once he became aware of who had taken his daughter he would attack his village. So the men of the tribe began to prepare for war.

He watched his son become more distant and withdrawn. He needed him to help lead their men. But no matter how many times he tried to talk to him, Ioopu, no longer recognized him.

At the same time Erangue's men were preparing to confront Ramanmada's tribe. There had been many meetings between the different tribes and alliances were made with the two confronting tribes.

The women of the village wove thick woven body armours, which would cover all of a man's body. They wove helmets; some had shells woven into them to make them stronger. The armour would help stop the clubs and knives from penetrating deep into the body.

The men set about making spears; some with long serrated sides made with the bones of sharks. The clubs had either sharp lime stone tips or thick shark teeth. They made axes with clamshell blades and spears made from the strong tomano branches.

Erangue's armour was more elaborate than the

other men. The helmet was larger, it was woven so as the top of his head was covered in a high oval cone. A finer weave was worn underneath, with flaps down around his neck to his shoulders. He also wore a shield that covered all of his back and straight up over his helmet. He stood out from the other men. The black feathers of the frigate bird sewn into his helmet indicated his *position* within the tribe; he was their chief.

The women of the village were afraid, but they wove the thick body armours.

The men were busy preparing for conflict and so they did not go out to the deep sea and fish to feed the tribes. It was the women and children that had to collect more coconuts and fish from the reef. The village had become ominous of the impending war.

Ekewane was unaware of what was happening when she was in her unconscious state. But when eventually she did wake up and understood what was happening, she cried; the blood of her people that she had seen was to come about – and it was because of her.

She tried to talk to her father, but his honour was at stake and she knew that he would not abandon his plans.

Then one morning the news had come. Ioopu was dead. Someone had entered his hut and killed him, all eyes were on Erangue, now Ramanmada was not only defending his tribe but it had become a 'blood vengeance' - there would be no peace from now on.

Erangue had the huts of his tribe that were scattered amongst the trees, torn down, and rebuilt close together in a circle. He then linked the coconut trees behind the huts with vines and branches; this he thought would help stop anyone creeping into the village at night.

And then the nights were filled with blood.

Enemy tribes creeping through the protection barriers would enter huts and kill indiscriminately; the sour toddy drink gave them courage and fuelled the men. The attackers often burnt the huts of their victims as they left the scene of devastation.

The bodies of the dead were quickly buried in front of the huts. A small rock would indicate the loss of a family member; now the rocks in front of the huts of the tribes around the island were numerous. The surviving members of the families lived in constant fear. It had become a guerrilla warfare; too afraid to go into the undergrowth and too afraid to sleep at night.

The men spoke about their attacks, or how they

wanted to be buried. Some men preferred to be buried at sea, so their enemies could not cut up their bodies, whilst others wanted to be buried the more traditional way, near their families. If an enemy was killed the body would be thrown out at sea, or in a deep cave.

The island that had offered shelter to those lost at sea was now killing them one by one.

Ekewane no longer met her friends at their special peaceful place; the boys were either at war or preparing to fight.

Erangue forbade any of the villagers to leave the village at night; it had become too dangerous.

And still the war went on.

Ekewane and Eiru, together with the other women worried about the men that went out at night, and for all those that remained behind; death was always a constant fear.

And still the war went on.

The number of people still alive on the island was now dwindling; soon there would be no more, as the tribes were determined to kill! Each family member killed had to be vindicated; so the killing would never stop, until all were dead.

As the weeks and months went on Ekewane became more anxious for her people.

They had all belonged to one tribe in the beginning. They had all faced the perilous sea to get here; and now they were killing each other. They had forgotten why they initially started the war. She knew that the sour toddy annihilated the men's sense of reasoning.

She prayed with her mother to the spirit world to stop the carnage, but the spirits of the island ignored them.

"Maybe they do not want us here, this is their island and they want us to destroy each other," she often thought to herself.

One night she heard the men of her village talk about an attack on Ramanmada's village, their allies would also be present, they would be in great numbers they reasoned.

Ekewane saw Emarr and his tribe present, she no longer recognised him. He was now a leader, one of the men that commanded respect.

"He has changed, he is no longer the same shy Emarr. I do not know him anymore," she whispered to herself, and as she whispered these words Emarr lifted his gaze to her as if she had called him. He looked at her sadly and then returned his attention to the other men.

Months had passed since the four friends had sat in their quiet peaceful spot watching the waves.

"Emarr and Bagonoun are my friends, what will become us all? Will we all be killed?"

Ekewane felt angry! She had never been this angry in her life.

"Foolish men!" She yelled. Only the wind and the spirits heard her.

As soon as her words came out, the screaming from the mountain spirit shrieked out as if to confirm the plan that had begun a few nights before, and was now taking form. She knew that she would probably be killed, but if her life could save her family, Emarr, Eiru and Bagonoun and her people, then she was willing to sacrifice herself.

"It is my fault that the war began and now I must try to end it!" she said to herself.

But her words were braver than she felt. "What can I do? I am only a girl." Her eyes burnt, but the tears this time would not come. For the first time in her life she felt defeated, "If I am not killed first, I will have to watch our people die one by one," she lowered her head and began to chant a sad and mournful note, it was not one of her mother's chants, but come from deep inside her. It was a chant of loss and despair.

Ekewane looked around confused. She was still very small and sitting around a fire with other members of her tribe. Emarr and Anweb, her childhood friends, were sitting by her side. She looked over and saw her mother holding her dead baby brother Debao!

"Where am I?"

She was sitting on soft warm sand. She recognised the feel of the sand so different from the limestone reef, "this is my island! I am home!" she said out aloud.

"I have been dreaming about the new island. There was so much pain and suffering there. Angry spirits lived on that island." For a moment she felt relief flood over her; it was just a dream!

She looked more carefully. There was something strange about the scene. "Where is the other Emarr, and Bagonoun? Did I dream of them too?"

Ekewane looked at the tribe sitting there around the fire listening, so she listened to see why they were all so enthralled.

An old woman sat near the fire at the centre of the circle. Her voice like a whisper, but everyone could hear her. The old woman Wahema was the storyteller of her tribe. Ekewane remembered her, the children looked forward to the nights when Wahema would tell of their beginnings, their legends and myths, and also of their heroes. Ekewane sat there and listened attentively, the legend was about a woman named Rahene, she was the chief.

Rahene had lived a long time ago, in a time when there were many killings with the neighbouring tribes. And it was Rahene's brave sacrifice that stopped the killings, she had stood in front of the two fighting tribes and lifted her hands in the air and called upon the spirits of their ancestors to stop the senseless killings. Someone had thrown a spear and killed her. Rahene was also a great sorceress, she could contact the spirit world, and so the spirits would now vindicate her death; the tribes were terrified, there was no protection for anyone against the fury of the spirit world, they had seen it before. The sea had rose up like mountains and flooded many of the villages, then there were many years when no rain had come and they went hungry, and there were years when the fish had disappeared. So the tribes put down their weapons and went back to their villagers and prayed forgiveness to the spirits.

Ekewane woke up startled; confused again she was back on the dark island. The spirits had taken her back to when she was on their island and she understood why. It would be difficult and dangerous but she could not bear to see any more of her people die. Death no longer frightened her, she knew that she would join the spirit world- she had been there many times and this thought gave her the courage she would need.

The next morning with the excuse to look for octopus holes she kept walking further along the reef. Nobody took any notice of her and she kept pretending to fish, and all along moved further away from her village. She soon came to Emarr's village and was afraid that he would be there, but even in this village the people were too preoccupied to notice her.

As soon as she left Emarr's village she headed through the thick forest towards the mountain. She no longer felt afraid but determined to carry out her plan.

All day she walked. The mountain no longer seemed threatening compared to the hatred killings of the islanders, so she continued. As she walked she chanted her prayers to the spirit world to give her courage.

She remembered Emarr and Bagonoun that night they had rescued her, there had to be a cave with water somewhere. She could not remember where because she had been unconscious for most of the way. She felt thirsty and tired but kept walking determinedly.

It was late in the day, the green of the undergrowth became cooler and darker when she saw hidden behind two large boulders an entrance to a cave.

"The spirits are with me!" She said thinking she had found the same cave.

She hurried towards the opening, and then stopped

and listened, afraid that maybe others were waiting inside, and would kill her before she could complete her plan, she knew she would not be able to defend herself against any man. So she listened for a while, it was silent so slowly stepped in.

She was not sure if it was the same cave and cautiously walked into the opening. With a sinking feeling knew that it was different. The cave had a large entrance but then opened into two connecting tunnels. The limestone walls were encrusted with the bones of many fish and animals and she shuddered.

"What will I do?" she asked herself out loud.

She was afraid but knew that she would die soon anyway, so if the spirit world wanted to take her now, they would. So courageously went into the tunnel to the left. It was dark, a dim streak of light filtered through the main cave to the floor of the tunnel, so she followed the faint stream of light on the ground. Her eyes become accustomed to the dim light and she could see the sides of the tunnel. On the sides of the walls there were the exposed roots of trees, and coming down from the ceiling, were thin pointed rocks covered in a leathery dark green substance. The tunnel was not very long and it lead to a small chamber, in the centre was a small pond. Ekewane knelt down and drank thirstily.

Once she had drunk her fill, she ran back to the entrance of the tunnel to the main chamber. The hot air hit her with a whoosh! She remained stunned for a moment; it was cool in the cave. But she did not want to sleep there, so walked a little way ahead and found some branches where she sat down to rest.

"Emarr," she sighed, "if only he and Bagonoun were here with me," but then shrugged, she knew they would never have allowed her to carry out her plan.

After a short while she got up, she could not afford to sleep. There was a full moon that night as she stumbled through the undergrowth. She could see the silver rays coming down thought the breaks of the trees. She was no longer convinced she was heading in the right direction and could not go any further, her body ached and she was exhausted, so lay down to have a rest again, but quickly fell into a deep sleep.

A scream awoke her and she sat up startled. "The mountain spirits have awoken me, I must continue," she said out aloud.

The sun had started coming up over the horizon. The golden rays could be seen streaming though the overhanging branches.

Further along Ekewane could smell the smoke of the night campfires, they were not that far away; and she knew that she had arrived at Ramanmada's village!

As soon as she came closer and could hear the soft sound of water, she began to crawl until she came in sight of the huts, there she would wait.

The morning went very slowly as the people of the village continued their daily tasks, some of the men walked around the outer edge keeping an eye open for attackers. They did not see the small girl lying there under the cover of branches.

And Ekewane waited.

The sun was straight overhead and still there were no signs of her father, but she did not move. "He will come," she kept saying to herself.

When sthe un had started to set and the strange light of the tropical twilight bathed the village, she heard a scream – a warning and knew that her tribe was there.

It was going to be a full-on battle face -to -face, Erangue wanted to destroy all of Ramanmada's village, he had lost too many of his people to keep going with small skirmishes, now his attack would end with the death of one or both of the two chiefs.

The two tribes and their allies stood face-to-face ready for the order or any sudden movement before their killing frenzy would begin. Ekewane looked at the two opposing teams and ran out screaming.

"STOP! STOP!" Everyone looked at the girl bewildered.

Emarr recognised Ekewane and moved towards her, Erangue stopped him.

Ramanmada was about to throw a spear at the stupid girl, but stopped. The other members of the warring tribes also stood deadly silent, confused.

Ekewane closed her eyes listening to the frantic beating of her heart, expecting to take her last breath, the spear that would kill her, but there was only silence and so slowly peeked between her eyelids. The men stood there watching her. She felt the perspiration run down her body, she opened her mouth, but no sound came out. Then she remembered, the blood, all that blood that was always in front of her eyes when she closed them at night; the blood that ran in streams in her dreams - the blood of her people.

The anger within her started bubbling to the surface, she could not stop it, nor control it. She felt her body tremble out of control, and then lost all awareness of whom she was.

A strange eerie silence covered the village, the only sound to be heard was the screaming spirit mountain, but it too stopped.

"Ai! Ai ! Ai ! Our people are dying. We will no longer exist as a people. The spirits of your ancestors have asked you to stop! They will not forgive you if you do not listen to them. The blood vengeances will destroy you all!" Ekewane's voice was strange; it did not sound like her young voice but that of a very old woman. Ekewane had been in a trance and once the final words were uttered, she dropped to the ground.

It was Emarr who threw down his spear first, and then Erangue, Ramanmada and the other men also laid down their weapons. their ancestors had spoken and they did not dare question the power of the spirits.

Erangue then walked towards his daughter and picked her up still unconscious. He then returned to where his tribe was standing, with his free hand picked up his weapons, turned around and walked away.

No one spoke.

Ekewane woke up hearing the sound of the waves crashing against the shore. Her father was carrying her.

Emarr and Bagonoun walked on either side of the bewildered girl and smiled at her. Every now and again her body trembled as they slowly walked home together.

Peace had come to the island again. The war had ended just as swiftly it had begun. The islanders went again about their daily lives. The dead whose bodies were buried in front of the huts had now become part of the spirit world and would be called upon to protect those that had survived. The villagers offered them food and coconuts as were the customs of their people since time began. Their ancestors were the guardians of the house and family, and once again they had saved them.

Ekewane, Eiru, Bagonoun and Emarr sat silently in the place that had been abandoned for many months. Nobody spoke, each contented to be there with each other. Emarr held Ekewane's hand and she again felt safe.

Erangue and Emanear were watching the four friends sitting together quietly.

"The spirits on the island have changed our children. One day our children will not be bound by our traditions. The time of asking the spirits of our ancestors to help us will end. When we are gone, our future children will not remember us. Our children will be lost without the spirits of our ancestors. There will come a time when they will seek other Gods because they will be confused and afraid. Our people will have to face many difficulties in the times to come and they will be lost."

Emanear looked up at her husband and he saw the tears running down her face. He laid his arm across her shoulders and they slowly walked back to their hut. He did not question Emanear. She had great magic within her, so he knew she was right and had foreseen the future of their people.

The old woman sat there silently, her eyes transfixed on the fire as if in a trance. All around her was silence. The group of people sitting around the fire knew that the story of their people for tonight, had ended, and soon the old woman would slowly get up and walk back to her hut. The story of their tribe would continue again another night. The children looked forward to this storytelling and the adults, although they had heard the stories before, would never be tired of hearing them. No one moved as they waited for the old woman.

Then she whispered: "The story of our people has been told and must remain told." Then stood up unsteadily, and staggered towards her hut.

*Island Village*

## Synopsis

Ekewane is a young girl on the brink of womanhood. For thousands of years her ancestors had lived on an island in the Pacific. However, due to years of drought many tribal members were forced to migrate in search of a new land in which to settle.

Ekewane is faced with fears of not only surviving on an unknown island, but her own feelings as she becomes a woman. On her quest she discovers powers within her that she has inherited from her ancestors. Ekewane forms a friendship with three other young people who are also faced with a fight for survival.

The story looks at the dangers and fears faced by islanders in their wooden canoes, as they travelled the vast unpredictable Pacific Ocean in search of new islands to settle. They take with them a culture embedded in magical beliefs, sorcery and mystical beings as they face unknown dangers with only their courage, and the belief in their gods and ancestors whom they pray to help them survive.

Tribal Classes and Clans

**Ramaoide** (elite members of the tribe)

**Eilu Clan**

        Great Head Chief Ekriaro - (grandfather - remained on island home)

**First settlers on Volcanic Island**

        Erangue  (father)    Emenear (mother)
        Ekewane (girl 12)    Enara (boy 8 )
        Equi (4)
        Daboi (baby boy-deceased)
        Gaida (uncle)    Erianga   (aunt)
        Eiru (girl 12 cousin)

**Enename**  (middle class )

**Iwa Clan**

        Ramanmada (father)  Enemame (mother)
        Ioopu (boy 16)    Emet  (girl 14)

        Gope   (boy 16 Ioopu's friend)
        Ludi (girl 14 Emet's  cousin  and friend)

**Sitio** (lower class members of the tribe -slave like position)

**Kalab Clan**

        Roqua  (father)    Gorube  (mother)
        Emmar (boy 16)